"I want t
but she's

"It's okay, Connor. You can plant them with
another time," Torryn said, turning around in the car
to pat the little boy's leg.

Connor slumped against the back seat. She looked
at Matthew, expecting an explanation, but he was
staring straight ahead, hands tightly wrapped
around the wheel.

Torryn couldn't figure out what she had said wrong.
Matthew whispered, "His mother passed a couple
years ago."

She gasped. "Oh, I'm sorry. I had no idea." All of a
sudden, everything made sense. She apologized
again and Matthew reassured her, but Torryn was
concerned about the little boy, who had suddenly
become solemn and withdrawn.

"I'm sorry your mom isn't here, Connor."

His chin quivered. "Who's going to plant sunflowers
with me? I don't have a mom."

The words tore at her heart. Taking control of the
situation, she said, "We'll plant them together,
sweetheart."

Zoey Marie Jackson loves writing sweet romances. She is almost never without a book and reads across genres. Originally from Jamaica, West Indies, she has earned degrees from New York University; State University of New York at Stony Brook; Teachers College, Columbia University; and Argosy University. She's been an educator for over twenty years. Zoey loves interacting with her readers. You can connect with her at zoeymariejackson.com.

Books by Zoey Marie Jackson

Love Inspired

The Adoption Surprise
The Christmas Switch
The Family Next Door

Visit the Author Profile page at LoveInspired.com.

THE FAMILY NEXT DOOR

ZOEY MARIE JACKSON

LOVE INSPIRED®
INSPIRATIONAL ROMANCE

ISBN-13: 978-1-335-93729-2

Recycling programs for this product may not exist in your area.

The Family Next Door

Copyright © 2025 by Michelle Z. Jackson

For questions and comments about the quality of this book, please contact us at CustomerService@Harlequin.com.

® is a trademark of Harlequin Enterprises ULC.

Love Inspired
22 Adelaide St. West, 41st Floor
Toronto, Ontario M5H 4E3, Canada
www.LoveInspired.com

Printed in Lithuania

MIX
Paper | Supporting responsible forestry
FSC® C021394

It is of the Lord's mercies that we are not consumed, because his compassions fail not. They are new every morning: great is thy faithfulness.
—*Lamentations* 3:22–23

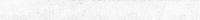

To my husband, John. Thank you
for your faithfulness as a man of faith. Your touch
grounds me. Thank you for your never-wavering
support as I pour out these stories of my heart.

For my son Eric, continue to depend on God's
faithfulness as you strive to be the best husband
you can be to Jasmyn and provide for your
daughter, Nova Jade. For my son Jordan, may you
find peace in God's love as you wait patiently
for God's healing and the one God has for you.
To my sisters, Zara, Chrissy and Sobi, may God
enlarge your territories. To my parents, may God
grant you peace. To my prayer-crew fam, Arlene,
Paula and Andrea, thank you for your faithfulness,
your consistency and your support.

Thank you to my editor, Melissa,
for her understanding and for helping me
get this manuscript into the book it is today.
Thank you to my agent, Latoya,
for her continued support with my career goals.

Chapter One

One of the biggest luxuries of being in business for yourself and living in a small town like Ryder Hill, Delaware, was that you could take your child with you to work, and no one would think anything of it.

After his wife, Eloise, had died from MRSA two years ago, Matthew Lawson struggled with being a single father to his now four-year-old son, Connor. If it hadn't been for his mother, Peggy, he didn't know how he would have managed. But unfortunately, it seemed like he was about to find out. His mother had left for Florida the day before, to care for her ailing sister, so Matthew had lost Connor's sole caretaker.

Leaning against the white countertop in his kitchen, while Connor ate his strawberry-and-cream oatmeal for breakfast, Matthew gripped its beveled edge as he pondered his situation. He needed to seek out a replacement babysitter because as the town's leading estate attorney, he had just accepted a big case that could go to trial and he couldn't take his son to court. He glanced out the large bay window past his backyard and groaned at the overgrown grass of his neighbor's yard before redirecting his vision to the white cabinetry with carved trims that Eloise had specially ordered yet never fully enjoyed.

He sighed. Everything was so different now that she was gone.

"I'm finished, Daddy," Connor said, seated on one of the four stools around the oversized kitchen island. Matthew looked at his watch and shoved off the counter. His appointment should be arriving soon.

Matthew's heart expanded at the sight of his son's stocky body, the shock of brown-and-blond curls and those hazel eyes, which peered back at him with such trust.

"Okay, we've got to get going, buddy. Put your bowl in the sink."

He washed Connor's hands and then inspected his son's outfit. He had dressed Connor in a pair of khaki shorts and a blue-and-white-checkered shirt. Almost an exact replica of what he was wearing, except he had on pants. Seeing no stains, they headed out the front door. Sweeping his gaze across the neat lawn, rounded box-wood shrubs and Japanese maple, he eyed the flower bed. He needed to work on pulling those weeds.

Just then, a cyclist swerved to a stop next to his vehicle. Taking off her helmet, she tossed her strawberry-blond hair streaked with gray before saying, "Hey, Matthew. I'm glad I caught you. I left my key on your kitchen counter."

"Ms. Anna!" Connor squealed.

"Hello, Anna," Matthew said, greeting his house-keeper, a retired pulmonologist. Anna had a car but pre-ferred to ride her bicycle to his home since she only lived a couple miles away. "Yes, I put it on the key rack for you."

She had rung his doorbell a month after his wife's passing and had said, "My rates are good and you're going to need me."

And she had been right. He had hired her on the spot and had no regrets. If only Anna's services extended to child care. Matthew retraced his steps to let her inside his home.

"Thank you." She gave Connor a tight hug. "See you later, Little Man."

"Bye, bye, Ms. Anna."

Making his way down the paved driveway once more, Matthew settled Connor into the booster seat in his black Ford Expedition and headed to his office. He put on some children's music to entertain his son during the twelve minute ride to his office located in the heart of the town.

Connor was busy singing along, moving his body to the tune, leaving Matthew free to worry about his lack of a babysitter. Should he have his administrative assistant rearrange his appointments for the next few days? He rubbed between his eyes, feeling every day of his thirty-six years. Connor bellowed out the final word of the current song, which made Matthew smile and hum along. Connor stopped singing and looked at him, unsure.

Matthew tensed. "It's okay, buddy. You didn't have to stop singing."

Connor dipped his chin to his chest. "I know, I just..."

"You just what?"

"Nothing..."

Gripping the wheel, Matthew hated how his commu-

nication with his son was so stilted, unnatural and awkward. He wiped his brow. He was a master at talking to
people and adept at handling emotional situations. His
job as an estate attorney required a certain skill set that
worked with everyone but his own child. Connor only
clung to him when he was around strangers, or scared.
The rest of the time, his son appeared uncomfortable
to be in his presence, and Matthew had no clue how to
fix that.

When they arrived at his office, Connor maintained
a tight grip as they walked up the gravel path and ven-
tured inside. As he stepped through the door, the light
lemon scent teased his nostrils. Judging by the fresh
lines on the carpets, the large sparkling windows and
dust-free ceiling fans, it was clear the cleaning crew had
dropped by the night before. The yellow fabric chairs,
the coffee table equipped with a charging station and
the tea-and-coffee station made the reception area in-
viting along with the smiling face of his assistant. He
greeted her with a wave, eyeing one of Eloise's abstract
paintings behind her desk, before making his way into
his private space, which consisted of his oak desk with
a makeshift play area for Connor behind him, a conference table and a large SMART board.

He took a few minutes to set them both up for the day,
reminding Connor to play quietly with his action figures
and LEGOs while he welcomed his first client of the day.

By the end of his third appointment, Connor had gotten a dollar and a lollipop from Matthew's clients. His
son had built a fortress and was enacting a scene with
himself as the superhero.

Before Eloise's passing, Matthew had been too busy

building his business to spend much quality time with his family. It was something he deeply regretted now that his wife was gone. But he had no idea how to mend that bridge. Especially when it came to Connor. If it hadn't been for his mother and his faith, he would have sunk under the weight of his grief and despair.

As it was, he had shied away from attending church services, not wanting to see the pity on everyone's faces.

Connor let out a giggle.

Turning his head to glance at his only child, Matthew smiled. Connor lifted his head to look at him before returning to his toys. Grey eyes were a heritage of most of Matthew's relatives who lived in Accra, Ghana. Connor's pupils were hazel like his mother's. That difference sparked the debate around Connor's paternity with his mother and his nana, Afia. In a moment of weakness, during a weekly video call with his nana who had then told his mom, he had confided that Eloise had had a brief affair. Now, they were pushing Matthew to find out the truth.

He didn't care or need to know. In every way that mattered, Connor was his son. Case closed. But when his mother had mentioned the possibility of Connor needing a blood transfusion or something, he had caved and gotten a DNA test.

The results had come yesterday, but he hadn't looked at them yet. His mother had been on the phone with him for a good two hours trying to convince him to open the letter.

With a sigh, Matthew turned to look at the clock across the room.

It was almost time for the Emerson siblings to arrive

for the reading of the will of their adoptive mother, Ruth Emerson. Theirs was his last appointment of the day. He moved from behind his desk and walked over to the conference table to retrieve the remote. Then he pressed the start button to turn on the SMART board. He would mirror the document from his computer to the screen so that he could provide any explanations if needed.

Ruth had shared that her baby girl, Torryn, was spunky and resourceful, which was why Ruth had been sure Torryn would be up to the task she needed her to do. Ruth had also stated that Torryn tended to ask a lot of questions. But he was prepared.

After pressing the intercom, Matthew asked his assistant to bring in the folders for the Emersons, along with bottles of water and a few of the homemade chocolate cookies with caramel she had brought in.

Suddenly, he heard a thud, then Connor ran over to him. He must have dropped his toys when he saw the cookies. "I want a cookie, Daddy," he said, having inherited Matthew's love of sweets.

He placed a hand on Connor's shoulder to keep his son from snatching one of them. "These are for Daddy's clients. How about some nice crunchy grapes instead?"

Connor pointed. "Can I have the cookie? Please?"

"It's *may* I have the cookie."

Jumping up and down, his eyes bright, Connor said, "*May* I have a cookie, please?" He pointed to the largest one. "I want that one."

Matthew couldn't resist that little face with those chunky cheeks. He wrapped the cookie his son had asked for in a napkin, then gave it to him, along with a bottle of water. He hoped it wouldn't ruin Connor's appetite for lunch. Then again, his son was always hungry. Just like Matthew had been at that age, according to his mom.

Hearing voices outside his office, Matthew checked the mirror to his right to make sure he didn't have anything in his teeth before buttoning the top button of his dress shirt. He had worn short sleeves this morning, since the temperature was in the upper seventies—awesome for mid-May—and he wasn't due in court today.

The Emerson siblings entered and Matthew greeted everyone and gestured for them to sit around the conference table. Once seated, the trio introduced themselves. Though they were very different, Matthew could see shared physical traits that showed they were biologically related as well as being adopted siblings. Tess was the eldest and petite. Even with her heels, Tess barely reached her brother's chest. Nigel, who was bulky and broad-shouldered, eyed him with a slight frown, and then there was Torryn. The photos of Torryn that Ruth had shown him didn't compare at all to the real thing.

She was beautiful.

As soon as she sat down, Connor called out, "You look like my mommy!" then rushed over to Torryn and jumped in her lap. Torryn froze, her mouth hanging open.

Matthew felt his cheeks burn. "Please, forgive my son," he said, then he called to Connor, who was now playing with her hair.

She waved a hand. "It's quite alright. He's adorable."

Torryn did look a bit like his late wife. Both women shared the same large eyes and high cheekbones, though Eloise's face had been more rounded and Torryn's was more angular. And her eyes had been hazel, while Torryn's were a light shade of brown. And, of course, there was the difference of their skin tones. Eloise had been white, while Torryn was the color of smooth caramel.

But unlike Eloise, who had barely topped out at five feet, Torryn was taller, leaner and there was a distinct variation in their style. Eloise would never leave the house unless her outfit was coordinated and well put together. Torryn, however, was dressed in a wrinkled T-shirt with a picture of a woman with an afro printed on it, which she'd tucked into a pair of dark jeans, and wore the brightest neon-green sneakers he had ever seen. But the main reason Connor had found Torryn similar to Eloise was because of her hair, which was like his late wife's—faded and short on the sides, with a glorious mess of curls on top—in the picture of Eloise beside Connor's bed. The only picture of her he had up in his house.

Torryn grabbed two cookies, biting into one with gusto, then sneaking the other to Connor. With a loudly whispered thank-you, his son returned to play with his toys.

"First, let me say that I'm sorry for your loss," Matthew said. "Ruth Emerson was loved by many here in Ryder Hill, including me."

"Thank you," Tess said. "People used to say there wasn't a stray cat, hungry dog or thirsty bird that Ruth didn't feed. And that included foster children like myself and my siblings, whom no one wanted."

Matthew handed out copies of the will, guiding them through the important sections. He was especially worried about them getting to *that* part.

Torryn's head popped up first. "Three months? She

wants me to live in her house for three months? I was thinking that we would put the house up for sale or something…" Her expressive eyes went wide, and she was already shaking her head. Then she read on, and eventually commented, "Seems like I will be the first." She tilted her chin at Nigel and Tess. "Then it will be both your turns."

"Wait. What does that mean? Mom wants all three of us to live in her home for three months each?" Tess squeaked, running a hand through her natural curls. "What am I supposed to do with my apartment?" Tess was the only one of the three who had never left Delaware.

"Are there any more directions from Mom about all of this?" Nigel asked.

Matthew nodded. "Ruth couldn't decide who should get the house, so she stipulated that each of you spend a set amount of time there, with a certain task to do. She left letters for each of you to read at specific times."

Having visited the property many times before her death, Matthew knew the main house wasn't habitable because it needed repairs, but Ruth had renovated the guesthouse.

"Sorry, I don't need the money that much." Nigel dropped his copy of the will on Matthew's desk. "I have prior commitments and, frankly, I just don't want to be in Ryder Hill."

Torryn jabbed her brother in the chest. "Oh, please! You would do anything for Mom, so I don't believe it has anything to do with 'prior commitments'." She used her hands to form air quotes. "You just don't want to come back here because of—"

Nigel cut Torryn a frosty look.

Tess raised an eyebrow. "Torryn. Leave it alone."

Matthew wondered what that was all about, but his job was to focus on fulfilling Ruth's final wishes. He gestured to Tess, and asked for her thoughts, but was somewhat distracted by Torryn tapping her leg. She had a restless energy about her.

Suddenly, Torryn jumped to her feet to pace the room, and began drumming her fingers along her chin. She made a beeline to Connor. He could hear her talking with his son in a kid-friendly voice. From the sound of it, Connor was lapping up every word she said.

After a few beats, Tess spoke up in a soft tone, recapturing his attention. "I'm happy to do it after all Mom did for me, and if I'm being blunt, that money will help me with the foundation I want to start."

"A foundation?" Torryn asked from behind him, then scurried to sit in another chair at the table.

"Yeah, that's the first I'm hearing of this," Nigel said.

Tess shrugged. "It's nothing I want to get into right now." Her tone suggested that whatever her plan was, it meant a lot to her.

Matthew sat back in his chair. He had been in many meetings with families before and knew it was time to remain silent. He often had to wait for heirs to process the wishes of their loved ones, while also grappling with their grief. It could get volatile and he was prepared to play referee, but Matthew never forgot that his sole purpose was to enforce his client's will.

"I'm knee-deep in debt right now," Torryn said, back to her foot-tapping. "So I could use the money. I want to get back to Philly, but I don't have a place to live, so I guess I'm stuck here until I figure out my next move."

Her siblings' heads whipped toward her. Matthew noted she didn't look the least bit embarrassed. In fact, she met each of their gazes with a defiant look.

This was getting personal. Matthew made a move to stand. "Why don't I give you all a moment to talk alone?"

Torryn waved a hand. "Oh, please. There's no need. I'm an open book."

Matthew couldn't imagine baring his personal life in front of a stranger like that. Both his parents were notoriously private and the nature of his business required privacy as well. As an attorney, he had to weigh every word before he spoke.

"What happened?" Nigel scowled, making Matthew wonder if the man ever smiled. His face was granite serious. "Last I heard, you had started a home-organizing business."

"I got sick. A ruptured appendix—"

"What?" Nigel interrupted. "I can't believe you didn't let us know about something so life-threatening."

"As you see, I'm alright. Now, back to my story." Torryn exhaled. "I was in the hospital when Brenda—um, that's my business partner—ran off with the money and shirked our clients. The police are investigating but they told me not to hold my breath. For all they know, Brenda could be in Albuquerque or Aruba by now."

Nigel whistled.

Tess's mouth dropped open. "That's horrible." Then she shook her head. "See, that's why I hate the big-city life."

"Small towns can have con artists," Torryn dryly returned.

"Yes, but we know who they are," Tess said, her voice steely, giving as good as she got. Matthew was getting a clear picture of what the Emersons must have been like as children. Ruth must have had her hands full.

"Carry on," Nigel said, waving a hand with barely concealed patience. Ruth had called him the middle-man, the mediator.

"Yeah, so Brenda left me with angry customers. I have a ton of bills to pay, and my landlord was quick to put me out." She rubbed her eyes, and Matthew detected a sense of doubt for the first time since she'd started spewing her misfortune.

Connor came over and touched his arm. "What's up, buddy?" he asked his son.

"I've got to go to the bathroom," he said, squirming and hopping from one foot to the other. Matthew should never have given him that much water to drink.

Matthew grabbed Connor's hand and stood. "Excuse us, but I've got to take my son to the restroom, but please take this time to decide—"

"Dad-d-y-y!" Connor squawked.

"Coming, son." He inched toward the exit, Connor jumping higher with each step. He spoke fast, trying to sound as professional as he could with a frantic child crying out next to him. "You should know that if you don't all agree to her terms, all the money will be donated to various charities. There is no splitting it between one or two of you. It's an all-or-nothing kind of deal." With that, he grabbed his son in his arms and sailed through the door.

* * *

"The pied piper of children strikes again," Tess said, as soon as Matthew left the room.

Torryn patted her recently dyed blond curls and rolled her eyes. "That was years ago." When she was a teenager, she had made extra money watching the neighborhood children and had been well liked as a youth counselor at summer camp. But those kids had been a good five years older than this little boy.

Tess snickered. "I don't know how he expects us to take him seriously when he's got a son wriggling in his arms."

"Poor Connor looked like he was about to burst," Torryn added, feeling a mix of commiseration and humor. She wasn't a parent, but she understood Matthew's plight. Connor was an absolute delight, so cute in his khaki shorts and shirt. She desperately wanted to squeeze those rosy cheeks.

Her brother smirked. "The poor man looks frazzled," Nigel said. "Why isn't his son at a sitter or with his mom?"

"I don't know," Torryn responded as she looked at her siblings, and her heart warmed.

It had been a long time since they had shared a laugh together, she realized. The last time had been at her mother's sixtieth birthday party ten years ago. Ten years. Though it felt like it had only been yesterday. Thinking of her mother, her smile waned. Placing a hand on her mouth, Torryn's chest tightened. "She's gone. Mom's gone and she's not coming back."

Ruth Emerson was the second mother she had lost in her lifetime. The first had been a month before her sixth birthday. And though both deaths had been heart-wrenching, this one definitely hurt worse than the first. Ruth hadn't been forced to take in a scrawny, mischievous soon-to-be kindergartner who still needed to be potty-trained. But she had. Ruth then poured so much love into her, nurturing her, that Torryn wished she had done more to make her proud. Wished she had tried harder to become the daughter Ruth had wanted her to be.

She'd always been weighed down with the guilt of her underwhelming achievements. Her sister was a social worker, and her brother was making a name for himself as an architect. Torryn was a high-school dropout, who'd hopped from job to job before finally opening a business as a home organizer. Then, when her appendix ruptured, her business partner, Brenda, ran off with her profits, leaving her penniless and evicted.

She hadn't bounced back from all that yet.

Ruth Emerson had left this earth when Torryn was at her lowest: broke, recovering and homeless. She had used the last of her savings to get to Ryder Hill. She sat there sniffling, wading through the deep waters of regret engulfing her sense of loss. A month before she died, Ruth had called Torryn and told her how much she believed in her, urging her to come home and start over, when all Torryn wanted to do was wallow.

After the funeral, Nigel, Torryn and Tess had gone to Tess's house, talking for hours, until Nigel went to the only hotel in town and Tess had turned in. Torryn had bunked out on Tess's couch.

"I know it sounds like a cliché, but at least she's at peace," Tess said softly.

"I know, but MRSA, you guys? MRSA?" She flailed a hand. "I don't get it. She was the fiercest person I know. She took in three of the worst kids in foster care and dragged us to church every week kicking and screaming. We were known as TNT for a reason. Mom survived our teenage years, getting hit by a car and even a cancer scare. But a random cut on her hand took her out. It makes no sense." Tears poured down her face. "It's ridiculous. A stupid cut and she's gone." Covering her face with her hands, Torryn sobbed.

Nigel put his arms around her. "I know it's hard, Torryn, but Mom wouldn't want us to grieve so hard."

Torryn used her T-shirt to wipe her face, and tried to compose herself. "I need to read my letter. I need to hear what she had to say to me."

"Me, too," Tess said, thumbing away a tear, before opening one of the bottles of water. Throat feeling dry, Torryn followed suit.

Nigel snagged a couple of tissues from Matthew's desk and handed them to her and Tess. "As soon as Mr. Hotshot returns, I'll ask him."

As if on cue, Matthew reentered the room, without Connor.

When Nigel asked about the letters, Matthew unlocked his cabinet and retrieved a single envelope. Then he walked over and handed it to Torryn. She tilted her head back, registering how tall and lean he was, especially standing next to Nigel, who was angling for his letter with a stern look on his face. Matthew didn't seem daunted by her brother's imposing presence.

Handing her the letter, he said, "Read that alone."

Then he faced Nigel. "You'll each get your letter when it's your turn to stay in the house."

The men engaged in a silent stare-down. To his credit, Matthew didn't flinch. Then Nigel held out his fist. The men fist-bumped before Nigel went to pick up his folder.

"I've a flight to catch, but I'm in. I'll go next if that's cool with you two. Lisa is in the middle of wedding planning and I promised I'd be there to help," he said, referencing his long-term fiancé.

Cracking up, Tess asked, "Are you really getting married this time? You two have been engaged for years."

"Yes." Nigel's face reddened. "I'll see you both soon."

"Tell Lisa we said hello." Torryn blew him a kiss, then called out, "Have a safe flight."

"Text the group chat when you get home," Tess added. Her sister had started a text chain to "promote increased communication" between the three of them. That had been Tess's phrasing. The queen of extraneous words, she never said anything simply if she could embellish it.

Just then, Matthew dangled a key ring holding two shiny metal keys. "Do you want the keys to your home?"

"*Temporary* home," Torryn corrected, her stomach in knots. She clutched the letter to her chest as she got to her feet.

"I've got to get into the office," Tess said, sliding her purse onto her shoulder. "But I can drop you at my apartment and take you to Mom's later if that works for you, Torryn."

With a nod, Torryn struggled to hide her disappointment. After seeing her biological mother die because of a bad car accident, Torryn was afraid to get behind the wheel. Many didn't understand why, at the age of twenty-eight, she'd never learned to drive, but many hadn't gone what she had gone through at six years old. That's why she had left town when she turned twenty and moved to major cities like Baltimore and now Philly. Public transportation.

"I could swing by there on my way home, if you'd like," Matthew said. "Ruth and I are actually neighbors. I bought the house next to hers about a couple of years before Connor was born."

"That's a great idea. Let me go cool the car down while you decide," Tess said as she strolled toward the door. Knowing her sister, her mind was on the children. Tess was one of the few people who loved what she did for a living. It had taken Torryn close to twelve years before she had found her calling. Cleaning up other people's messes, since she wasn't good with handling her own.

Torryn looked at Matthew. He appeared to love his job, too, but he seemed...uptight. "Don't you have appointments?"

"You were my last one for the day," he said. "It's up to you." Maybe *reserved* was a better word for him than uptight. Even now, his face was impassive, expressionless. Torryn didn't know if that was his personality or a persona he put on for his job.

She hesitated for a moment. She didn't know Matthew like that. But Tess didn't seem concerned with Torryn riding somewhere with him or she would have said so. To his face. Plus, he had a son, whom she presumed would be traveling with them as their unofficial chaperone.

"Thanks for the ride. I'll let my sister know." She sauntered out of the building, the heat smacking her in the face. She sputtered, wishing she had brought the rest of the water. Tess had already backed her sedan out of her parking spot and was waiting near the entrance. Torryn jogged over and yelled, "I'm going to catch a ride with Matthew."

After giving her a thumbs-up, Tess drove off. Seconds later, Matthew emerged with Connor beside him.

"Yay, are you coming with us, Tory?" Connor jumped with delight.

Before she could answer, Matthew placed a hand on his arm. "That's Miss Torryn, please."

She smiled when Connor ran over to her after making his way down the building's concrete steps. Those curls bobbed on his head, some covering his eyes. He wrapped his arms around her thighs and hugged her. In one swoop, Torryn hoisted him onto her back, causing Connor to giggle.

He shouted, "Whee! Go, horsey, go."

"Are you sure you want to do that?" Matthew asked.

"I got it," she said, her back slightly bent. "Lead the way."

Without another word, Matthew pointed to his SUV and unlocked the doors. Torryn marched over, wiggling and jerking her body to keep Connor laughing. To hide her awkwardness from riding in close proximity with a man she barely knew, she engaged with Connor while they drove. Torryn didn't remember Matthew from when they were kids. Probably because he'd been a few years ahead of her in school.

Soon, he turned onto her old street and her childhood home came into view. She sucked in a breath as she took in the familiar gravel path, the slightly overgrown lawn with perennials lining the long driveway. Both Tess and

Torryn had helped Ruth plant the flowers. She remembered the days had been hot and sticky and the chore tedious, but somehow Mom had made it fun.

To her right, she took in the small patch of sunflowers near the fence of her mother's yard. Connor pointed. "Look, Daddy. Those flowers are so big."

Torryn told him how she had planted those with her mom.

"I want to plant flowers with my mom." His face fell. "But she's not here."

"It's okay. You can plant them with her another time," Torryn said, turning to pat his leg.

Connor shook his head and slumped against the back seat. She looked at Matthew, expecting an explanation, but he was staring straight ahead, his knuckles white, hands tightly wrapped around the wheel.

Torryn couldn't figure out what she had said wrong. It wasn't until they had pulled up in front of Ruth's two-story home that Matthew whispered, "His mother passed a couple years ago. That's how I connected with Ruth. My wife and Ruth both had MRSA and though we knew each as neighbors and from church, their illness brought our families together."

She gasped. "Oh, I'm sorry. I didn't know. I had no idea." All of a sudden, the details slipped into place. Matthew and Connor had come alone to her mother's homegoing service. Connor had a play area in Matthew's office. She apologized again and Matthew reassured her, but Torryn was concerned about the little boy, who had suddenly become solemn and withdrawn.

As soon as they vacated the SUV, Torryn rushed over

to him. Bending her knees, she dipped her finger under Connor's chin. "I'm sorry your mom isn't here."

His chin quivered. "Who's going to plant flowers with me? I don't have a mom."

The words tore at her heart. Torryn had been only a couple years older than he was when she lost her biological mother. She had been hurt and confused. And she had spent many nights crying and many days looking out the window, waiting for her mother to come back and take her home. Feeling helpless, she twisted to face his father. Matthew stood with his hands jammed in his pockets, looking like he wished he could be anywhere else but there.

Taking control of the situation, she cupped Connor's head in the palms of her hands. "We'll plant them together, sweetheart."

Chapter Two

Matthew hardly knew what to say. Torryn should not have done that. She should not have made a promise that she might not keep. Connor had squealed with glee at her words before running to play at an old dollhouse and kitchen in a corner of the family room.

Now, he was going to have to deal with Connor asking him every day about planting flowers with Miss Torryn. Of her three children, Ruth Emerson had classified Torryn as a dandelion: free and untamed. Which to Matthew meant hard to pin down—as in, for all her good intentions, Torryn wouldn't keep her word to his son. Those were the thoughts reverberating through his mind the entire time Matthew stood inside Ruth's house, ignoring the overwhelming heat, waiting for her to read the letter.

But he said nothing. Because if he called her on it, she might say he could have jumped at the opportunity to plant the flowers with his son himself. And she would be right. He should've chimed in. To be fair, Torryn had given him a chance to do so. But he had said nothing.

More and more, Matthew was realizing that as Connor got older, his son would feel the impact of losing his mother at a tender age. And there was nothing Mat-

thew could do to prevent that from happening, which
made his heart hurt. There would be no photos at Connor's high-school graduation wearing a big smile as he
stood between both his parents. No mother to bug him
to clean his room or tease him about his first crush. No
mother to help Connor plant sunflowers...

Only a carefree young woman who was probably already regretting her brash offer. He stood several feet
behind Torryn, who had sat down at the large table in
the dining room and then torn open the envelope. It was
a large space with a painting of Ruth and her three children from her sixtieth birthday party, an event he had
missed because he had been away on his honeymoon.
The table was covered with an eyelet tablecloth and had
an empty vase, a sign of Ruth's absence.

Torryn's eyebrows knitted as she intently read the
letter. She dabbed at the tears in her eyes and then appeared to read it again. Matthew knew the contents of
each of the three letters because he had helped Ruth by
typing the small notes for her and then having her sign
her name.

The air was muggy, stifling. The house so still. He
could feel the sweat lining his neck and loosened the
top button of his shirt. Peeking over at his son, Matthew could see that Connor's hair had flattened with
perspiration. Torryn's forehead was beaded from perspiration. Matthew marched over to open the large windows. Almost immediately, the curtains fluttered in the
wind. The house hadn't been occupied in months, as it
was deemed uninhabitable, and he berated his thoughtlessness. He hoped there was something refreshing to
drink out in the guesthouse. It would take a few hours

to cool the house but he was sure that Torryn would appreciate it.

Matthew sat down across from her.

She looked incredulous. "Mom was about to lose this land *and* her house?" She waved the letter. "I had to read it twice to make sure my eyes weren't deceiving me. Can you explain to me how this happened?"

"When your mother fell sick, your sister began to manage the utilities and other incidentals. Tess didn't know about the property taxes. Your mother was old-school. She was used to going into the bank once a year to pay the taxes with Mr. Fischer. But when she was so ill, it was the last thing on her mind. By the time I stepped in to help her with her estate, the house was already in foreclosure because of all the back taxes. It goes up for auction in about three months, and it'll be sold to the highest bidder, starting with the amount owed."

Torryn jumped to her feet and paced, her curls bouncing with each step. The heat had made them more tamable somehow. "Are you telling me that this place—one of Ryder Hill's historical landmarks, with fifty acres of land and a guesthouse which my mother devoted her life to—might be sold for about six thousand dollars?" He nodded, adding that the neighbor on the other side, Blake Whitlock, had already indicated his interest. Her eyes flashed.

"That is just plain senseless. This house is worth way more than that."

"Yes. And if it does go up for sale, I'm sure there will be multiple bidders. But your mother had the faith that you would keep that from happening."

"I only hope her faith is justified and I don't let her down."

Sliding a glance Connor's way, Matthew was impressed with how quiet he was being. He had what looked like tiny green action figures in his hands that Matthew suspected had been Nigel's at one point. Matthew warned him not to put the toys in his mouth. Torryn walked over to fluff Connor's curls.

Connor wrinkled his nose. "Ew, that's disgusting, Daddy. I wouldn't put these in my mouth." His voice echoed in the house, so, of course, his son had to repeat it again.

Matthew and Torryn chuckled. "He sounded just like my mom just now," Matthew said. "He nailed her attitude and tone to a tee. I should have recorded it because she'd get a kick out of it," he said.

After placing the letter on the table and running her fingers through her hair, Torryn said, "Not everything has to be viewed from the other side of a lens. Some things are good to just experience, keeping a snapshot in your mind. Then all you have to do is close your eyes—" her eyes fluttered closed "—and soak in the memories." Then she smiled. A wide beautiful smile that seemed to light up the woman inside.

Connor stood and mimicked her actions. Matthew found himself speechless. But only for a second. When her eyes popped open, he said, "That was deep."

She lowered her chin to her chest and rubbed the bridge of her nose, a rosy hue painted across her cheeks. Interesting. Miss Open Like a Book had a shy side. There was also an old soul underneath her flighty exterior. Substance. Depth. *Potential.*

He was beginning to see why Ruth had chosen her to save the guesthouse, and now even Matthew believed Torryn had the ability to meet Ruth's request. And it was a big one.

Connor headed to the kitchen, where he picked up a thick, yellow fake fry and pretended to eat it. Matthew glanced at his watch. It was almost lunchtime. He knew his son was going to be asking for the real thing soon.

He cleared his throat and redirected the conversation. "What about the rest of what she said? How do you feel about that?"

"I don't know what to feel, to be honest with you. My gut reaction is fear. No, that word is too mild. What I'm feeling is sheer and utter terror and Mom insisted that I can't tell Nigel or Tess about the financial status of the house." Walking back to the chair she had vacated, Torryn hunched her shoulders.

She picked up the paper, and began reading out loud. "'My dear, sassy daughter, I need you to use every ounce of creativity you possess to save my house. I know your first instinct will be to ask your brother and sister for help…'" She paused to grin at him. "Mom knows me too well." Torryn continued. "'But I want you to do this on your own, without their help. Use your resources and keep my house off the auction block. And, to answer your question, I didn't fall behind on purpose. But I wouldn't be your mother if I didn't use this opportunity as a teaching moment. Because I believe in you, and I have enough belief to cover your disbelief. I know you will keep this land in Emerson hands because you are un—'" Her breath caught. "'Unstoppable. So get to work.'" Tears streaked down her face and her body shook with silent tears. "I don't know if I can do this. Her faith in me is misguided. She should have just asked you to pay the taxes."

"I tried but she was adamant... and she was in so much pain, I didn't push," Matthew choked out. He rushed out to the SUV to get napkins from a fast-food joint to bring them to her. After thanking him, she blew her nose and dabbed at her eyes.

Connor ran over to her and tapped her leg. "Why are you crying?"

She touched Connor's shoulders and looked him in the eyes. "Because my mommy died and that makes me really sad."

Connor's face fell. Matthew worried that he was going to have an inconsolable kid on his hands.

But to his surprise, Connor took her hands in his. "Don't cry, Miss... I forget your name."

"Torryn," she said as she wiped her face with the back of her hands.

"Oh, yeah, I forgot." He gave her a cherubic smile. "Don't cry, Miss Torryn, because guess what?" He leaned in and whispered, "My mommy died, too, but she's with God, so Daddy said we should be happy for her." Matthew swallowed hard to keep from breaking down at his son's words. Connor tilted his head. "Is your mommy with God?"

"Yes, she is."

"Then you get to be happy for her." Connor patted her on the back like Matthew had done for him so many times before. Torryn covered her face in her hands. Matthew got misty eyed as well.

"Do you want my daddy to sing for you?" Connor asked, his little brows furrowed.

"Buddy, I'm sure that's the last thing Miss Torryn needs right now."

"But, Daddy, Mom Mom Peggy says you can sing sing."

She gave him a skeptical glance. "He doesn't look like he can sing to me. He looks *way* too serious."

Seeing the mischief in her eyes, Matthew jumped to his feet and stepped outside to keep from falling apart in front of this stranger. Or worse, having to sing for her to please his son. He soaked in the sun while he thought about Connor. To see his grieving boy, who had nightmares most nights crying for his mother, try to comfort someone else was humbling. He was so proud of Connor, he thought his heart would burst. Scanning the vast land, he took in all the sounds and smells of summer around him. He drew in several deep breaths, then returned inside to finish the task that was his duty as Ruth's attorney to perform.

"What do you plan to do?" he asked her, secretly relieved to see Connor had returned to playing in the kitchen.

Her eyes were glassy, and he saw her shiver, but her voice was firm. "I plan to do my mom proud. I've always been…impetuous. I dropped out of high school the last semester of my senior year for no good reason." Tapping her chin, she said, "Well, in hindsight, I think it was fear, and I'm embarrassed to say I don't even know what I was afraid of." Lifting her chin, she said, "I think it's time I settle down long enough to prove to myself that I have staying power. I'm going to save her house. I don't know how, but I will. I have to."

Her resolve touched his heart. Looking at his son, who was also without a mother, he could feel his chest tighten. A mother's love couldn't be duplicated. He was sorry Connor would never be able to experience that. Unless…he started dating again.

But just as quickly, he shunned that idea. The last woman he had trusted had damaged that trust. Eloise's deception had been heartbreaking. That was why his mother and grandmother had insisted on the paternity test. So it would be foolish to even dip a toe in the waters. But…

When Matthew was about eleven, three years after his father's passing, his mother had gotten him a mentor. A big brother. Maybe he could do the same thing for Connor? Was there a big-sister program? Then he zoned in on Torryn, who was sitting next to Connor on the floor and playing with him. His mother's departure for Florida had left him without a caretaker for Connor. Maybe…

Nope. He'd think of something else. He was sure if he thought about it some more, the right solution would come to him. One that didn't involve a beautiful woman with cocoa-butter skin and blond curls.

Torryn wiggled her fingers so Connor would loosen his grip a bit as they walked toward the lake in knee-high grass, with Matthew trailing behind while on a phone call with a client. But the little boy was holding on tight as he stomped his way through the blades. Not that she minded. She had always gotten along well with young children. It was the adults in her life that she struggled with. Particularly men. They always seemed to misjudge her because she was a high-school dropout. Never mind that it had been by choice.

She shifted her thoughts from that subject to the matter at hand. Torryn had grown up in this house. And her mother wanted her to see the extent of the repairs needed, and it was a lot. Like *a lot* a lot.

The main house needed work due to age and a powerful storm that had left substantial damage to the roof. From the outside, the house appeared the same as she remembered it, with the chipped beige paint, the wrap-around porch and creaky boards, but the inside needed gutting down to the frame. It was a metaphor for her life. She needed a complete reboot. According to Matthew, Ruth had moved into the guesthouse with the intention of getting the work done, but then she had fallen ill.

They finally arrived at the lake, and she looked out at the calm waters. Connor bent down to pick up some pebbles to toss them in. She couldn't resist the opportunity to show him how to skip them on top of the water. Of course, that led to fifteen minutes of trial and error.

Having ended his call, Matthew tried a couple times to skip stones before giving up and shoving his hands in his pockets. Torryn encouraged him to take videos and photos of Connor's pebble-skipping adventure.

"When are we going to plant the sunflowers?" Connor asked, wiping his hands on his shorts and peering up at her while shielding his eyes from the sun.

"Really soon," Torryn said patiently, though it had to be like the sixth time he had asked. She hoped Matthew wasn't displeased at her spontaneous offer, and she sidled over to him to apologize.

He waved a hand at her. "I do wish you had asked me first, but I get it. It's not like I jumped in to volunteer."

She had wondered about that. He had looked ill at ease at the possibility. "Why didn't you?" Just then, her stomach grumbled. It had to be close to one o'clock, hours since she'd wolfed down those two cookies. She needed to eat.

Matthew must have heard her tummy because instead of answering her question, he asked her if she needed a ride to grab lunch and some groceries.

"I don't want to put you out," she said.

He pointed at Connor. "I'm sure my son is hungry but is too excited to notice. I think he would be thrilled if you joined us for lunch. If you aren't doing anything, that is."

Rubbing the bridge of her nose, she accepted his offer. "Great," he said. "It's a plan."

They started toward the guesthouse. She was so glad she had worn sneakers, but they were now blackened with mud. Stealing a glance at Matthew's shoes, she rolled her eyes. Somehow they were impeccable.

"You like having plans, don't you?" she asked, flicking off a blade of grass from her T-shirt.

"Yep. I thrive on stability." She noticed how he always kept an eye out for Connor, who was now running ahead of them, chasing a crane.

She snorted. "I'm the complete opposite. I run from routine so don't ask me how I ended up in the home-organizing business."

"Maybe a part of you enjoys creating structure out of the chaos."

"I certainly don't run from it. Chaos, that is. It always seems to find me."

"Yet, you're still standing."

The admiration and certainty in his tone was too much. It made her feel...awkward. She blurted out, "I had to file for bankruptcy."

Matthew stopped and placed his hand on her arm. "Don't do that."

"What?"

"Don't negate a compliment by pointing out your mistakes." He took a breath, then went on. "Simply say 'thank you.' And accept it."

She rubbed her arm where he had made contact. "It's too soon for you to judge my character."

"I disagree. When it comes to first impressions, his instincts are spot on. I trust his judgment implicitly."

Who was singing her praises? She knew it wasn't her mom, because Matthew had said *his*, not *her*. Her curiosity was piqued. "Whose instincts?"

"My son's. Children have a good sense of character. Connor loved your mom and he's taken a shine to you." He cleared his throat and dipped his chin to his chest. "That's why I'd like to make you an offer."

"What kind of offer?"

"I'd like to offer you a job. Something short-term that I think would meet your immediate need. And mine."

She arched an eyebrow. "What do you have in mind?"

"Would you be interested in being Connor's baby-sitter?" Before she could answer, he lifted a hand and went on. "It would just be until after the summer. He's already signed up for preschool starting mid-August. I had planned to take him to work with me but there might be times where having a child around could be inconvenient, like when I have to go to court. I have an estate case coming up and I can't take him with me."

Taking care of someone's child was huge. She would be responsible for Connor's well-being. Her stomach churned. But she needed the funds. How hard could it be? Connor was adorable, and like Matthew said, he did seem to like her.

She squared her shoulders and nodded. "I accept, but I've got to warn you my only experience with children is that I was a youth counselor to ten-year-olds at summer camp and I used to watch some of them on occasion. Just an hour or two. When do you need me to start?"

"Is tomorrow too soon?"

Chapter Three

*G*od worked fast. That's what Matthew reminded himself as he watched Connor take his bath that night, while the niggling doubts about Torryn floated around in his head. He'd prayed that very morning for help with Connor, especially since one of the two day-care facilities in Ryder Hill was only for children up to two years old.

After Eloise died, Matthew had enrolled his son in the other day-care facility but Connor had cried all day. The program manager had tried to be patient, but after two weeks, she had been frazzled and the other children disturbed. So she had told Matthew to pick up his son. Hearing Connor screaming in the background, Matthew hadn't argued, and the manager had asked him not to return.

That's when he had turned to his mother. Mom was a retired teacher, and she'd been fantastic with Connor, even teaching him how to sight-read word books. But now, his auntie in Florida had gotten sick, and his mother had to go take care of her sister. However, he had been stuck.

So he had prayed this very morning for assistance and God had answered.

But still, he was worried.

Torryn wouldn't have been his first choice. But he consoled himself with the knowledge that he was right next door and that Connor liked her.

"I get to see Miss Torryn again, Daddy," Connor breathed out, pumping his legs in the bubble bath. Matthew had filled the tub with a bit too much water, so, of course, there was spillage. "Is it time yet?"

"Yes, you will. But, no, it's not time yet. It'll be after you go to sleep and wake up." Matthew got to his knees and started fishing the bath toys out of the water and into the netted hammock secured with suction cups on the wall of the tub. He could feel the water soaking through his pants. In hindsight, he probably should have changed out of his dress clothes before giving Connor his bath.

"Oh. Do I have to sleep one time or two times?" Connor tilted his head back to look at him.

Matthew's heart melted. "Just once. Now, let's get you into your pajamas and you can brush your teeth and we can say our nighttime prayers." Connor jumped up, causing a big splash of water to hit him across the chest. "Whoa, take it easy, big guy."

"I'm sorry, Daddy." Connor lowered his head and hunched his shoulders.

"It's alright. It's only water," Matthew said, pulling Connor into his chest. His shirt was now wet but it was worth it when Connor wrapped his arms around his neck. Matthew returned the hug. "Let's get you dried off."

Matthew scurried to grab a towel from the hook behind the door. It was green and blue and had a hoodie with spikes, so, of course, Connor had to emit a large roar. After some cajoling, Matthew finally got Connor ready for bed.

Both of them were now on their knees in Connor's room, which was decorated in a dinosaur theme with lots of blues and greens.

"Can we add Miss Torryn to our prayers?" Connor asked, his head resting on Matthew's arms.

"Um...sure," Matthew said. He hadn't seen that question coming, but he knew the best way to handle it. "You can pray for her."

Connor gave a grave nod before closing his eyes. It was a good thing that Connor knew his prayers by rote because Matthew kept replaying Connor's request in his head. He tucked his son into bed and headed down the hall to his own bedroom. He needed to process what adding Torryn to their prayers meant for his son. The only other women they usually mentioned were his mother and grandmother. Adding Torryn to the list was a big deal. But maybe he was overthinking it?

Just then, his cell phone vibrated in his pants pocket. It was a text message from Torryn. They had exchanged numbers after she had agreed to babysit. Forgot to ask what time I should expect you.

For a brief second, he was tempted to tell Torryn he had changed his mind. But he had to go to court tomorrow afternoon for a probate case and Connor would be disappointed if he didn't get to see Torryn.

We will come about noon, he texted.

Great. See you then.

After entering his room, he rested his cell phone on the charger on his nightstand, his eyes falling on the Bible there. Matthew had recently purchased a new one, which featured topical studies and a timeline for reading the whole Bible in a year. He readied himself for bed, then settled onto the edge of the mattress before checking on the chapters he needed to read that night. A few minutes passed before he realized he hadn't registered any of the words, so he put down the Bible.

God deserved his undivided attention, and at the moment, his mind was preoccupied with the letter resting on the mahogany dresser to the left of his bed. After Eloise's passing, Matthew had decluttered the bedroom, painted the walls beige and decorated the room in soft browns. Then he had purchased a chaise longue, and a desk and chair that provided him a great view of the lush scenery outside. His bedding was plush and comfortable. He'd consciously created an oasis in his master bedroom. When Eloise had admitted her infidelity, that had been where they fought. Then she'd gotten sick and he'd cared for her in their room. So when she'd died, he had needed a change. He also had a stern rule that he wouldn't bring work in this space, and he had kept that promise to himself.

However, that envelope threatened his peace of mind, and messed with his sleep.

Groaning, he tossed back the covers, grabbed the letter and shoved it inside his nightstand drawer. However, out of sight didn't mean out of mind in this case. Restless, he strolled out of his bedroom, down the stairs and into the living room, the only sound the trickling of the indoor waterfall fountain, then headed toward the kitchen. Maybe a cup of chamomile tea would settle him.

The kitchen was the one room in the house he had left untouched since Eloise had already upgraded it. She had been an artist and had converted some of her abstract paintings into window valances. The bright colors provided an eye-catching contrast against the white cabinets and appliances. Putting on the electric kettle, he peered outside the kitchen window, which was dotted with raindrops from a light drizzle.

From his vantage point, Matthew could see the lights were on in his neighbor's guesthouse. He cocked his ears, picking up the strains of notes. Torryn had to be blasting the music if he could hear it. Then something caught his eye. Movement in the backyard. He squinted and leaned forward. The exterior lights were on and he could see a shadow jumping up and down.

Was that Torryn? Dancing?

Was she seriously dancing in the rain?

The kettle hissed and he hurried to pour two cups of tea, then placed them on their matching saucers and exited into his backyard to investigate. Walking past the large trampoline that he had yet to allow Connor to use, Matthew trudged across the wet grass, Torryn's hooting and hollering a welcome distraction.

"Are you trying to scare the squirrels?" he called out once he was close enough for her to hear him above the sounds of the music she was playing. She had gone way back with that one.

Torryn let out a squeal and placed a hand on her chest. "Oh! You scared me. Was I too loud? Sorry about that." She paused the music and bounced over to him, slightly out of breath, her eyes bright. Her blond curls were plastered across her forehead. "I didn't think you could hear me. I was sitting on the back porch, feeling sorry for myself, when I decided to put on one of my mother's favorites. This was her Sunday morning cleaning music and it boosted my spirits."

Matthew chuckled. "I know." The teacups rattled in his hands. "I brought you some tea if you'd like some."

"Would I ever. Thank you."

Following her lead, he took huge gulps of his tea. She gave him a warm smile, causing his chest to expand. Between that and the joy in her shining eyes, his breath caught. Then he blushed as he realized she'd said something and he had to ask her to repeat herself. Laughing, she said, "I was asking if Connor was asleep."

"Y-yes. He's excited to play with you tomorrow. You were his main topic of conversation tonight."

"No wonder my ears were ringing," she laughed. "I'm looking forward to it, too. I intend to order the seeds for us to plant flowers."

Relief filled him, but he added, "I hope you're ready for an energetic four-year-old. He can be a handful."

She flexed a bicep. "I was born ready." Then she took a sip of the tea before closing her eyes. "This is delicious."

"Your mom purchased these teas for Eloise—th-that's my, uh, Connor's mom, when she was ill." He quickly changed the subject back to Connor. "I'm taking the morning off to spend time with him before my court appointment tomorrow." He swallowed some of his hot tea to keep from confessing it was the first time in months he had taken time off from work.

"Aww. That's sweet. What do you plan to do together?" she asked.

"I have no idea," he said, feeling his face warm.

"I don't want to intrude, but how about I make you

guys breakfast before you have your adventure?" Before he could decline, she held up a hand. "Now, before you say you don't want to put me out, you wouldn't be. I could actually use a ride to the grocery store, and me making breakfast would be my way of thanking you."

He arched an eyebrow. "What's on the menu?" he asked, picturing Torryn popping frozen waffles or bread in a toaster.

"How about some cheesy biscuits or fluffy cinnamon rolls?"

Sweet tooth activated. He nodded with much enthusiasm. "I'd be happy—I mean, *Connor* would be happy—with whatever you choose."

Taking the last gulp from her teacup then placing it on its saucer, Torryn backed away with a small wave. "Awesome, I'll see you in the morning. I'll be ready by six."

When Torryn had lost her biological mother, she'd had no other living adult relatives to take care for her. Now, when she lost Ruth, at least she had her siblings—along with her mustard-seed-sized faith. Torryn sat on the porch a few minutes before six that morning with Ruth's Bible on her lap. Just running her hands across the worn leather provided her much comfort. It had been more than a minute since Torryn had gone to church, but she had Ruth to thank for helping her develop a love for God and His Word.

Ruth had tucked handwritten notes all throughout the pages of the Bible, and Torryn was enjoying reading the verses and affirmations. Her mother had been an amateur poet of sorts, and though she was gone, Torryn felt that she was still speaking to her through these words.

One in particular resonated with her: *Even a dying plant still has its roots, a promise of a second chance.*

Torryn dabbed the corner of her eyes. Ruth had seen the beauty in everything, and now she was gone, leaving a gaping hole in Torryn's heart. One that she didn't see healing anytime soon. The sound of tires on the gravel stirred her into action. She ducked into the house, the screen door slamming behind her, to place the Bible on top of all the unopened mail—mostly bills—on the small credenza, and to grab the flyer she had worked on. Then, after giving her curls a light toss and reapplying the coral lipstick that matched her shirt and jean shorts, she dashed outside, her sandals crunching on the pavement.

When she got into the car, Matthew grunted a greeting, then released a yawn. Torryn bit back a smile. Okay, someone was *so* not a morning person. Connor, on the other hand, was stretching his arms out toward her.

"Morning, Miss Torryn. Daddy said you're making us minnamon buns."

"That's right." She giggled. Since she hadn't yet bolted her seat belt, Torryn turned around to squeeze the boy's hands briefly. "But I'll need someone to help me spread the icing across the buns."

"Yum." Connor smacked his lips and rubbed his stomach. "I can do that." He was dressed in a polo shirt and another pair of khakis similar to the one he had worn yesterday. A little mini me of his father, who was dressed in the adult version of that outfit. Torryn wondered if Connor even had jeans and sneakers, but it wasn't her place to ask. While entering the vehicle, she had spotted an iPad attached to the rear of her passenger seat. Since

Connor was playing a cartoon, Matthew told Connor to put on his headphones.

She touched Matthew's arm and whispered, "I guess I should have asked first if you're alright with him helping me," just in case Connor could still hear her. The youngster was busy singing and clapping along with the video he was watching.

Matthew chuckled. "It's all good. He beat me to it."

"Miss Torryn, you're the best," Connor announced from the back seat.

"Aw, thank you, Connor. I think you're pretty amazing, too."

He smiled and returned to his show.

"It's barely been twenty-four hours and already you've got a number-one fan," Matthew said, grinning at her.

Laughing, Torryn relaxed into her seat. "I guess cinnamon rolls are the way to a little boy's heart."

"Not just his," Matthew joked as he turned onto the main road.

To keep herself from reading more into his words, Torryn looked out the window and started to make small talk. "It looks like they've built up a lot of the area since I've been gone."

"Yes, I think the only thing we're still missing is a great breakfast place. Remember the diner that used to be near the edge of town?" When she nodded, he said, "The place closed. I think they plan to tear it down and build a bank or something."

"Oh, that's too bad," she said. "Is the bakery that used to be across the street from the grocers still around?" Torryn asked. That's where she had done her baking internship, when she had entertained the possibility of be-

coming a pastry chef. She had been working on the final
course before completion when she'd quit. Because she'd
been afraid. Story of her life. That's why when she had
started her home-organization business, she had made
sure to get a partner. Someone to help hold her account-
able, but, of course, she hadn't anticipated that Brenda
would betray her like she did.

"The original owners retired, and it wasn't the same
under new management, so they finally closed their
doors a few months back. We could use a new bakery."

Her heart saddened to learn that it was gone. So many
changes… Maybe she should open a bakery instead. Just
the thought of that venture made her heart hammer with
fear. What if she failed at something she truly loved? It
was better to stick with the safer choice. Besides, she
needed to get back to Philly, or maybe she should settle
in Baltimore next. She tapped her fingers on the passenger door. "Since you work with estates, do you know
anyone that might need a professional home organizer?"

"Not at the moment, but I'll keep you in mind." He
glanced her way as he pulled into the town's grocery
shop. "Already regretting the babysitting job?"

"No, no," she quickly assured him. "I'm looking to
do both."

Matthew put the vehicle in Park. "I see… Why not
put an ad in the local paper?" he asked. "Though I doubt
anyone in these parts would want a home organizer. That
sounds fancy, like something reserved for the rich and
famous. Unless you work with hoarders?"

"My business is on a much smaller scale," she said.
"I haven't taken on any clients of that magnitude yet. I
thought about linking up with a professional cleaning

company but hadn't pursued it after I got sick. For now, I'm looking to work with widows, people ready to relocate or downsize. That sort of a thing."

"Okay, I'll keep it in mind for future reference. Maybe I can recommend you to my clients." He jutted his chin. "The offices for the *Ryder Hill Gazette* are right across the street from this store if you want to snap a picture of the number on your phone."

"That sounds like a great idea."

"Is home organizing your dream job?" he asked.

She shrugged. "It's a job."

While he went to get Connor out of the back seat, Torryn captured a pic of the paper and slipped her phone in her pocket of her jeans.

Next to the paper, she noticed the Closed sign on the front door of the bakery, Pattie's Pastries.

Memories of many happy mornings with her family flashed in her mind—Nigel and Tess sitting at the kitchen table licking the batter after Torryn "helped" her mother prepare the batter for the cookies. That was where her love for baking all began. Then she had served as an intern at that very bakery. She placed a hand over her chest, unexpectedly sad at the loss.

Realizing Matthew was standing by the open door waiting for her, Torryn shook off her doldrums, stepped inside Mr. Rodney's Grocers and waved at Mr. Rodney, who used to give her a lollipop every time she would come to his shop with her mom.

The first thing she did was put her flyer on the job board on the wall. She stepped back to read her handwritten advertisement for dog-walking services because, as her Mom would say, every dollar was part of a hundred.

Next, she grabbed a shopping cart, ignoring the squeaky left wheel. She knew from many years of coming to this store that there was no use trying to find a better one. There weren't any. She made her way down the first aisle, which had breads on one end and fruit on the other, with Matthew and Connor in tow. She placed some of each at the top of her cart.

"Wait up," Matthew said, coming over to put Connor inside the cart instead of in the child seat since he was a little too tall to fit inside the seat comfortably. She paused. She hadn't considered that Connor would need to be secured in the cart. But it made sense or he would run amok in the store.

"How about you push him in this one, and I use another?" she suggested. Matthew went back to the entrance to retrieve another cart.

"Miss Torryn, I want *you* to push me," Connor said, bouncing hard enough to make the cart move. She quickly grabbed the handles to keep it from tipping over.

"Alright, we'll see what your father says when he returns." Of course, Matthew agreed, making Connor move about even more. Chuckling, she made her way through the aisles and picked up flour, eggs, salt, cinnamon, yeast, sugar, milk, confectioners' sugar, vanilla extract, cream cheese, butter and brown sugar.

"Whoa, that's a lot of stuff," Matthew observed.

"You need a lot of ingredients when you're baking from scratch." She snapped her fingers. "I still need cheese for the cheesy biscuits." She headed back to the dairy section and picked up a couple blocks of cheddar cheese. Then she realized something. "Honey. I'll need honey and parsley." Torryn backtracked to grab those ingredients. By now, the cart was almost full. Plus Matthew had packed a few things in his cart.

"I didn't realize you would be baking the cinnamon rolls from scratch," Matthew said. "I'm more of an add-water-and-stir kind of a baker. Or, better yet, tear-apart-and-bake."

Torryn smiled. "I've been baking since I was about seven years old."

"You seem to be able to do a little bit of everything." His voice held a note of awe. "I saw your sign for dog walking."

She laughed. "Yes. My problem isn't skill. It's consistency." They made their way to the front of the store to check out.

"How are you going to juggle all these jobs if you get them?"

Was he worried that she would flake on her babysitting duties? "I plan to keep a tight schedule but taking care of Connor would be my main gig. Those are my side hustles. You might not need me every day, so…"

"Ah, okay." Matthew's eyebrows lifted. Torryn pulled the cart to the checkout counter.

When Mr. Rodney saw the items in her cart, he said, "I bet whatever you're making is going to be delicious." Torryn knew that was a hint and smiled. Her mother used to make baked goods to feed his sweet tooth all the time.

"I'll be sure to save you some."

"If it's no bother." He placed the items into brown paper bags as he rung up their order.

"None at all. I usually make extra, anyway."

Mr. Rodney rubbed his chin. "Maybe I can sell some

here, since Pattie's Pastries is closed." He pointed to his
empty display case. "I have the perfect spot for them if
you feel like making additional money."

"Sure. You'll have to come get them, though. I don't
have a car."

Matthew placed the bags into the shopping cart. She
could see him biting back a smile.

"Alright. That's easy enough," Mr. Rodney said. "Let
me go get you some extra ingredients. On the house."

Matthew insisted on paying for the other goods, despite Mr. Rodney's protests. And Matthew refused Torryn's attempt to give him cash, stating it was the least he
could do since she was making them breakfast. Torryn
didn't argue. Her low bank balance overrode her pride.

"I can't believe you ended up with a baking gig, and
you've only been here for a day," he said, putting the
goods into the trunk of his Expedition. "Plus, I'm pretty
sure you'll get calls for dog walking."

She grinned. "I gotta make money somehow."

"I gotta make money," Connor repeated.

"I see that." Matthew's tone held admiration. "You
are a woman of many jobs. And talents." He strapped
Connor inside the booster seat.

Torryn waited until they were back inside his car before asking him about his career choices. "What about
you? What did you want to be when you were growing
up?"

Connor must have thought she was talking to him because he replied, "I want to be an astronaut." Then he
mimicked the sound of a rocket blasting off.

"Oh, that sounds like a cool job, sweetie," Torryn
said, reaching behind her to ruffle his curls.

"Yeah. It is the most special one." Connor's chest puffed.

"I always knew I would be a lawyer. From the time I was Connor's age. Just like my father and my grandfather before him," Matthew said.

Her eyebrows rose. "Wow. That is impressive."

He jutted his chin toward his son. "I don't know if he will keep the family tradition. But I will certainly encourage it."

"Is it an expectation?" Torryn twisted her lips. She didn't know if she agreed with that, but who was she to argue?

"No, but it would be…nice."

Man, it seemed like this guy had no room for spontaneity in his life whatsoever. "So you never dreamed of doing anything else?"

Matthew shook his head. "No. Once it was decided, I remained focused until I achieved my goal. I graduated top of my class in high school so that I could earn a scholarship—though my parents had saved up for my college tuition. But I wanted to do it all on my own."

Torryn drummed her fingers and looked out the window. By the time she was twenty-five, she had tried out at least ten different kinds of jobs, including waitress, lifeguard, travel agent and medical billing. And she had started her certified nursing assistant certification, and beauty classes. The key word being *started*. She hadn't finished any of the courses, including pastry school. Matthew seemed…settled. Secure. Responsible. The exact opposite of her.

A feeling of inferiority washed over her. Compared to Matthew, she was…scatterbrained. She slid a glance

Matthew's way. He appeared to be deep in thought, his eyebrows practically meeting in the middle, his hands gripping the steering wheel. Maybe he was having second thoughts about hiring her. Not that she could blame him.

A little hand tapped the back of her seat and she turned around to look into Connor's smiling face.

"Do you have a step stool?" he asked.

"No." She bit her lower lip. "But we'll manage."

Matthew chimed in. "You can always bake in my kitchen. I'm pretty sure I have every gadget known to man thanks to..." Torryn figured Matthew was referring to his wife, but it appeared that talking about her was difficult for him.

Just then her phone rang. It was someone asking about her dog-walking fees. Putting her best customer-rep voice on, she pulled up the calendar app on her phone.

"Thanks for offering the use of your kitchen," she whispered once she was off the phone. "Are you sure you don't mind me puttering around in your wife's space?"

"I don't mind. My housekeeper, Anna, comes in three times a week to clean so I just have to let her know. She actually prefers to prepare my meals at her own place. So, it's no problem at all."

Chapter Four

While Torryn was negotiating her dog-walking schedule and prices with the prospective client, Matthew wondered how she was going to manage so many jobs. Torryn was determined to honor Ruth's wishes and though she had assured him that Connor would be her top priority, what if she decided to quit watching Connor because she became overwhelmed?

Maybe he needed to put an ad in the paper for a babysitter as well. Just in case.

Then he scolded himself. She had given him no reason not to trust her, and if Miss Ruth believed in her, then so should he. Matthew knew that since Eloise's betrayal, he struggled with trusting others. Particularly beautiful women.

Not that Torryn's physical appearance mattered when it came to Connor's well-being. But when he looked into those expressive brown eyes of hers, it was hard not be taken by her earnestness.

He checked out Connor in his rearview mirror. His son was looking out the window and naming the colors of the other cars as they passed by. Then Connor asked Torryn how to make the buns, which she began to explain in such a fun way that Matthew wished he could join them. He told himself it was because of the sweet treats and not because of the woman sitting next to him.

Just as he parked in his driveway, Torryn's cell rang again. Thinking it might be a potential customer, she answered the call on speakerphone.

"Miss Emerson? I am reaching out in regards to your overdue hospital bill. Good news—we found funding to take care of a significant portion of your balance. But you're still responsible for fifteen percent and we'll need to make some sort of payment arrangement to keep your account from going to a collection agency."

Though her cheeks reddened, Torryn didn't take the phone off speaker. She tucked a curl behind her ear and said, "Um, yes. I am more than happy to work out a payment plan for what I owe."

Deciding to allow Torryn some privacy, Matthew opened his door and lifted Connor out of his car seat. Then he grabbed a couple of the grocery bags from his trunk and took them inside.

"I can help, Daddy," Connor said, holding up a hand. Looking down into that trusting face just made his heart melt.

"Alright, buddy, you can carry this for me," he said, giving his son one of the lightest bags. There was a crack of thunder, followed by raindrops.

He opened the garage, then walked through it and into the entrance leading to the kitchen while keeping a close eye on his son. Besides the Emerson property, their nearest neighbor was Blake Whitlock of Whitlock Farms. The quickest way to get to Blake's property was a cut-through on Ruth's land. The trail was about a half-mile long. There was also a creek between Matthew's and Ruth's land and Connor loved to play in the water, especially when it rained. A few times Connor had taken off running toward the water bur Matthew had snatched him just before Connor hit the mud.

He saw Torryn walking in behind them, lifting a couple of bags of groceries. He was pleased when he heard her gasp.

"This kitchen is like a baker's dream." Placing her bag down, she said, "There are two ovens in here. *Two.* This is like something you'd see on a cooking show!"

He chuckled to himself, then said, "Yes, we used to entertain a lot back when..." Clearing his throat, he stepped out of the kitchen to get the rest of their items. For some reason, when he was in Torryn's presence, he spoke about his late wife. But he had to be mindful of Connor. The last thing he wanted was for his son to have more nightmares. The less he spoke of Eloise, the better.

When he returned to the kitchen, Torryn asked him, "Would it be possible for me to see my mom's financial documents? I want to get a good understanding of the tax situation with her land so I can grasp what's ahead of me." She didn't bring up the phone call with the hospital, so Matthew didn't pry. Seeing a twig in her hair, he retrieved it from her tresses.

"Sure. I actually have her files here so I can gather all the financials and we can talk after I've had my meeting." Once he had put all the food away, Matthew went into his office to make a conference call with the other attorney on the probate case. He could hear Torryn and Connor laughing together, and it lightened his heart. When was the last time he'd heard so much laughter in his house? It was evident that Connor liked her. And he did, too. As his son's caretaker.

His office mainly consisted of his desk and his library, which had law books and crime thrillers along with the romances Eloise had liked to read. He'd kept them because his mother also loved that genre. In the corner of the room, there was a piano keyboard. He hadn't touched it in months except to dust it on the days when Anna didn't come in.

Hearing a tune in his head, Matthew walked over and touched his hands to the keys. After clearing his throat, he started to sing, then quickly stopped. He was way too rusty. Shaking his head, Matthew made his way toward his desk to prepare for his call.

Once it concluded, he proceeded to retrieve the documents Torryn had requested from his briefcase. His cell phone rang.

It was Blake Whitlock. He had a pretty good idea why he was calling. Matthew and Blake had graduated from high school the same year. He came from a wealthy family, and though Blake wasn't at the level of his parents' snootiness, he was a shark when it came to getting what he wanted. Like he had wanted Eloise... But she had chosen Matthew.

"Hey, Mattie, I wanted to put in a bid for the Emerson house when it goes on sale. When does the bidding start?"

Ruth had barely been buried and here he was swooping in like a scavenger. Matthew gritted his teeth to keep from snapping at Blake's thoughtlessness. "It's not for ninety days." He quickly added, "Ruth has family,

Blake. They're going to try to save the property before that happens."

"Oh, well, I can always see if they would be interested in selling." He laughed. "And I wanted to give you a heads-up that I plan to contest Ruth's property line marker. It extends five inches into our territory and it's time to claim what is rightfully ours."

Matthew frowned. "This is the first I'm hearing of a property line dispute."

"Yes, my daddy tried to get that fixed before he passed, and I promised I'd do it for him."

"I can respect that. But I'll be working toward Ruth's house and land staying in the family."

"Do what you have to, and I will do the same." He hung up soon after.

Matthew pinched the area between his eyebrows and exhaled. Picking up the paperwork, he walked back into the kitchen. What he saw there made his mouth drop open. Thirty minutes and his kitchen was...unrecognizable.

Even Torryn, with her hands deep in kneaded flour, had to acknowledge that Matthew's kitchen was pristine no more. Flour dusted the floor, cheese dotted the countertops and there was sticky residue across her shirt. However, Connor was enjoying the experience. His chin and face were covered with flour, cinnamon peppered his hair and he was licking powdered sugar off his hands.

Matthew's mouth dropped open, his eyes scanning the once immaculate space.

"I know this looks terrible," she said, not the least bit apologetic. "But Connor is having the time of his life."

His house was gorgeous, structured and...stagnant. Like living in a display case. The only things missing were the Do Not Touch signs. It was hard to believe a four-year-old lived here. Where were the crude finger paintings haphazardly taped to the refrigerator? The muddy shoes from too much playing in the rain?

"It looks like a category-three hurricane passed through here."

"I'll have it spotless in no time," she promised.

Matthew sniffed the buns that were sitting out on the counter, cooling right next to her first batch of biscuits. Then he pinned those gorgeous gray eyes on her, making her insides squirm like gummy worms. She was sure her face was flushed. "They smell amazing."

"Thanks." She turned away so he wouldn't see how pleased she was at the compliment. "I'm waiting on your son to put the icing on the buns and then it will be time to eat."

Connor stomped into the room, bopping his head from side to side. His shirt was wet and grass-stained and he had a rip in his shorts but his eyes sparkled. Torryn's heart expanded and she smiled. She ruffled his head and explained, "We were in the backyard on the trampoline as the cinnamon buns were baking. Connor said it was his first time."

When Matthew didn't respond, Torryn turned to face him.

Her eyebrows rose when she saw his face filled with quiet fury. Matthew's fists were clenched at his sides. "You shouldn't have done that without asking me first," he said, then stuffed his hands in his pockets.

Her heart raced, but Matthew just stood there. He

was visibly trying to get control of his emotions. Torryn racked her brain but couldn't figure out what she
had done to upset her new employer. She needed this
job. Badly.

Connor pulled on her T-shirt. "Are we going to ice
the minnamons now?" he asked.

"In a minute, honey." She took one of the buns out
of the pan and placed them on a paper plate before giving Connor some of the icing to spread on top. Connor
immediately stuck his finger in the goo to taste. Torryn
remained very much aware and unnerved by the angry
man behind her. She went over to Matthew and placed
a hand on her hip. "What did I do?" she asked under
her breath so Connor wouldn't overhear their exchange.

He sighed before shaking his head. "Never mind, I
overreacted," he said, in a much calmer tone. "I had that
trampoline sitting out there for a good three months and
had yet to play with Connor on it. I can't fault you for
doing what I should have done."

The dejected expression on his face was almost her
undoing. "I agree with you. You waited way too long,"
she said. Matthew spoke the truth. That was a lot of time
to not give Connor a go at it. "Now I get why Connor
begged me to play on it with him." She patted Matthew's
arm, feeling the strength in his forearm. "But you can
still take him out to play on it after we're done eating.
He's four. I promise you—it will be brand-new to him."

Matthew narrowed his eyes. "I thought you said you
didn't know much about children?"

"I don't. I'm working off pure instinct here."

His face dropped. "Something I feel like I'm sadly
lacking at times."

"You'll be alright," she said. "Let's eat—" A loud clang interrupted her.

"Whoops," Connor said, a little tremor in his voice. "I'm sorry. I didn't mean to do that."

That didn't sound good. Both Matthew and Torryn swung around to see the batch of the biscuits scattered on the kitchen floor. Connor looked ready to cry. He gave his father a fearful glance. Placing a hand to her lips, Torryn couldn't keep her laughter at bay. "It's all right, sweetie. I always bake a lot, so I do have more bis-cuits. We'll feed those to the birds outside. Or maybe the squirrels will eat them."

"That's a great idea," Connor said, his face transform-ing into a smile. "The birds might be hungry." Then he looked at Matthew. "Right, Dad?"

Torryn hoped Matthew wouldn't reprimand him. She whispered a quick internal prayer for Matthew to show his son grace.

A moment later, Matthew cleared his throat and said, "How about I take you outside to see if the ducks are hungry? We can go see the mother duck and her babies by the lake." Torryn drew in a deep breath. Matthew sounded nervous, like he was unsure how Connor would react to his suggestion. Of course, she knew that it was a no-brainer and gave Connor an encouraging nod.

The little boy tensed his shoulders for a brief mo-ment before giving a serious nod. "Okay, but we've got to eat the minnamons bun first." He lifted his little face toward her. "I don't want to share those."

Torryn cracked up. "Yes, we can eat first." Matthew gave his son a thumbs-up while Connor jumped up and down. This little guy was pure joy. He was already claiming her heart and she was more than fine with that. She couldn't wait for their next adventure.

Chapter Five

"No! No. Mommy!" Connor screamed at the top of his lungs. "Mommy!"

Matthew bolted up and ran into Connor's room, his heart pounding in his chest. Seeing his son thrashing about on his bed, the sheet wrapped around his legs, Matthew rushed over to Connor's side.

"Connor, wake up, son. Wake up," Matthew said in a calm tone, while detangling Connor's legs from the sheets.

But his son was still in the throes of his nightmare, his third in the past week. His forehead was matted with sweat and tears streamed down his cheeks. "Mommy!"

"Please, son. Wake up. Daddy's here." Matthew lifted his top half and hugged him tight. "Connor, you're having a dream."

Connor's body jerked against his as he began to sob. "I want my mommy." The raw pain in his voice twisted Matthew's gut.

He patted Connor's back. "I know. I know. But Daddy's here."

Connor wrapped his arms around Matthew's neck and clung tight. "Don't leave me, Daddy. Don't leave."

Matthew scooped him in his arms while fighting back

tears of his own. "It's alright. I'm here and I'm not going anywhere."

After he finally calmed down and woke up, Matthew made Connor use the bathroom before they both made their way down the hallway to the master bedroom. Then he placed his son on the side of the bed that used to be Eloise's. Connor shot him with a trusting gaze before he yawned and closed his eyes. Seconds later, he was fast asleep.

Releasing a long breath, Matthew rubbed his eyes. The clock on his nightstand showed that it was just after five in the morning. He yawned, unsure if he could go back to sleep.

For a few minutes, Matthew sat watching the rise and fall of his son's chest while his stomach churned with turmoil.

Bunching his fists, Matthew stormed out of the room and went into his study, then he groaned. "Lord, I don't know how to be who Connor needs. If Eloise were here, she would know what to do, what to say. She was a great mother to him. So, patient and kind. Sometimes I wish You had taken me instead of—" He paused, then drew in a deep breath before he dropped to his knees. "I'm sorry, God. I'm grateful for the gift of life. But my son's heartache is ravaging my heart." Covering his face with his hands, Matthew pleaded, "Help me help my son."

Minutes later, he washed his face and headed back to bed. Connor's arms and legs were spread wide like a starfish. Despite his heaviness, he chuckled and situated his son back on one side of the bed. Hopefully, he wouldn't get a foot in his back or some such.

He didn't know how long he was lying there, looking

up at the ceiling, with his arms folded behind his head, when his cell vibrated. It was his mom.

Thinking of you.

How did she always know? Peggy always seemed to reach out whenever he most needed her. He gave her a video call. Though Connor was a sound sleeper, he kept his voice and call volume low.

"Did you open the letter yet?" were her first words.

He groaned. "Mom, I know you think you're helping. But this could hurt Connor, not Eloise."

"I'm helping you, Matthew."

"Mom, Connor's been my son for four years and no DNA results are going to change that," Matthew said, his eyes locked on the dark-skinned woman who looked more like his sister than the mother who had labored thirty-six hours to give birth to him. It was a fact she never let him forget. "You're the only grandmother Connor knows. Why would you take that from him?"

She sniffed. "That woman did you wrong and she's still doing you wrong even from the grave." If she could help it, his mother always avoided mentioning Eloise's name.

"Mom, I forgave Eloise because I couldn't have that bitterness transfer to Connor. He's the innocent in all this."

Peggy grunted. "I know and I love him, too. I just…" She shook her head. "I just need to know if Lawson blood flows through his veins. I need to preserve your father's legacy."

He sighed inwardly. Since his father's death, when

Matthew was eight years old, that had been Peggy's mantra. Stay in school to preserve your father's legacy. Get your law degree to preserve your father's legacy.

"I did all you asked of me," he said tenderly. "Since Dad's passing, I have been a dutiful son, haven't I? I want to be able to do the same for Connor."

"*If* he's your son. *That woman* broke her vows and betrayed your trust."

He rubbed his chin. "Mom, we keep going around in circles. The only reason you insisted I take the paternity test in the first place is because Nana said something. What would you have me do if he's not mine? Give him up? Place him in foster care? Because that's not going to happen. Ever."

Peggy ran her fingers through her waist-length hair, which didn't have even a single streak of grey, though she was fifty-eight years old. She raised an eyebrow. "But don't you wonder? Connor doesn't look like you." Her lips curled. "He's all *her*. He doesn't have our skin tone or even the signature Ibrahim trait," she said, pointing to her gray eyes.

Matthew leaned closer to the screen, his tone harsh. "If you or Nana have a problem with how my son looks, take it up with God. As for me, I'm about building a young *Black* man of character." He emphasized the word Black, because he knew his relatives had disapproved of him marrying a white woman, and he earnestly believed he was Connor's biological father.

Lifting his chin, Matthew recited almost verbatim what Peggy had told him often over the years. "Don't forget Nana had a problem when you married a man at twenty years old who wasn't Ghanaian and who moved you to the nowhere town of Ryder Hill, Delaware." He cleared his throat. "It wasn't until you had me that they finally thawed."

His mother put a hand to her long, regal neck. "Yes, well, you were the first grandchild and hard to resist. Plus, your father was a *faithful* man of God who took good care of us. Because of Simon, I graduated college without owing a dime. He was good with his money, and he left us well-provided for. How else could I retire from teaching at fifty-five?" He could hear the pride in her voice. "My mother couldn't help but love him."

Fortunately for Matthew, she then changed the conversation. "Have you found a sitter for Connor yet?"

"Yes, do you know Ruth Emerson's children?"

"I think so."

"Well, her youngest, Torryn, is watching Connor. She's living right next door in Ruth's guesthouse."

"Yes… I remember her now…"

He could only imagine where her mind was going. Peggy had been hinting that he should start dating again.

"If it's who I'm picturing, she's cute, isn't she?"

Torryn's face flashed in his mind—her quick smile, her sparkling eyes. Then he shook his head. What she looked like didn't matter. All that mattered was how she cared for his child. The last thing he needed was for his mother to believe he was interested in a relationship. But, if he was, it would be with someone who was more steady. Not so…spontaneous. Instead, he said, "Connor loves her."

"That's wonderful," she responded quickly. "She's sweet, though, isn't she?"

He inwardly groaned and ran a hand over his head.

He thought Torryn was beautiful, but there was no way he was going to admit that to her, and have his mother hoping for something that wasn't going to happen.

"Yes, she's good to Connor. But she's just watching him until he starts pre-K."

"Okay, I'd better go call your nana back."

Knowing his mother was about to report all that had transpired to his grandmother, he sighed. "Alright, Mom. Have a great rest of the day."

She blew him a kiss. "Open the letter, son. The truth shall set you free."

His mother was dead set on opening Pandora's box, when the truth was much better remaining buried along with Eloise.

Matthew reached for his phone, then called up his business calendar to view his schedule. He had an appointment with the son of a client in hospice at 9:00 a.m. The son, Lucas Brennan, refused to accept that his mother wanted the bulk of the estate funds donated to charities. Matthew was going to have a battle on his hands, and possibly a lengthy court case. Hopefully, Lucas would be able to come to terms with Agatha's—his mother's—decision.

With a yawn, Matthew closed his eyes.

It felt like he had just drifted off to sleep when his alarm went off. Jolted awake, Matthew reached over to see Connor had snuggled to his side.

"Hey, buddy," he said, standing up and giving his son a light shake. "It's time to wake up."

"I don't wanna wake up," Connor grumbled, his eyes still closed. "I wanna sleep."

After a couple more tries, Matthew said, "Don't you want to see Miss Torryn today?"

His hazel eyes popped open. "Miss Torryn?" Connor jumped up and out of the bed. "I want to go to Miss Torryn." He dashed to the bathroom.

Wow. Connor had grown attached to Torryn pretty quickly. Connor and Torryn got along so well. She felt like the perfect fit his family needed. He didn't know whether to be grateful that hearing her name got his son up and moving, or alarmed. What would Connor do when Torryn left Ryder Hill?

Matthew walked Connor out to the guesthouse, while he mulled on that question. When Torryn answered the door, Connor hugged her legs and promptly forgot about him.

"I'll be back by five p.m.," he said but neither of them acknowledged him.

Matthew's heart warmed but his worry at Connor's reaction to her departure intensified.

The next day, with her arms wrapped about her, Torryn stood by the doorjamb of her old room, the one she had shared with Tess. She had so many great memories here. She looked at all the papers, clothes and knick-knacks scattered all over the bed and floor.

Early that morning, she had been lying in bed thinking about what to make Connor for breakfast when Matthew texted that he wouldn't need her until noon. After having a cup of tea, she had dressed in a pair of shorts and a T-shirt, then walked over to the main house to check the mail and to assess the damage on the second floor for herself. It was disconcerting to know her mother, who had always kept a clean house, had started accumulating so many things.

Though the first floor of the house was decently clean, the four bedrooms upstairs were another matter. They weren't hoarder level, but there was a significant amount of stuff. In addition, the roof damage had led to water leaks in the master suite. Fortunately, Matthew said there wasn't any sign of mold, but he had placed buckets in crucial spots that she had to remember to empty if it rained. She massaged her temples. Before she could fix the roof, she had to get the bedrooms sorted out.

Torryn stepped inside and sat on the edge of the twin bed. This was as good a time as any to put her organization skills to use. She went downstairs to get a couple of trash bags from under the kitchen sink. Then she began sorting.

There was something soothing about making sense out of chaos. Though her mother had had faith that she would be able to figure out a way to save the house, Torryn had no idea where she would even begin. But she'd prayed for guidance and now she had to trust that God was going to lead her on the right track to figure it out.

It took a couple of hours for her to create several piles. One for donations and one for a potential estate sale. Some of the clothes still had tags on them. Torryn had ordered large plastic bins from the internet so that she could store some of her and Tess's memorabilia. If she could save this place—no, *when* she saved this place— she would redecorate. The first thing on her list would be to purchase a queen-size bed. Maybe she could talk to Tess about eventually making this into a bed-and-breakfast or something that could generate income once they were finished cleaning up the house. Unless, Tess wanted to use it for that foundation she wanted to start.

A sound in the distance captured her attention. Was that the doorbell? Yep, there was the distinct chime. She dusted off her jeans, then rushed down the stairs to answer the door. It was a deliveryman with a box of fresh fruit and vegetables. There was a small note from Tess.

How thoughtful. She placed the box on the kitchen table, then took out her phone and called her sister. "Thank you so much for the groceries, sis."

"You're so welcome," Tess said. "I'm sorry I haven't been by. It's been hectic at work, but I can bring you a casserole if you want."

"No need. I'm good. Besides, I know you have work to do. And I'm used to being on my own, remember?"

"Yes, but you're still my little sister and I want to make sure you're okay. How are you managing? I worry about you at Mom's house on your own without any transportation."

"Sis, don't forget I can use a rideshare app if I need to. Plus, I'm not alone… Matthew took me to the store so I was able to pick up a few things."

"Hmm, very interesting."

"What does *hmm* mean?" she asked as she sat in one of the kitchen chairs.

"It didn't mean anything." Yet the lilt in her sister's voice said otherwise.

"Nope. Whatever you're thinking, you need to unthink it pronto. If you must know, he asked me to babysit his son. That is all it is. I've been watching him since we met."

"Babysitting?" she scoffed. "How can you take care of someone when you yourself need taking care of?"

Torryn released a sharp breath.

"Oh, I didn't mean that *quite* the way it sounded."

Ouch. She had been plagued with the same doubts, but she was determined to try.

"It's sort of disappointing," Tess said, bringing Torryn's mind back to the conversation. "I was hoping you two would make a connection."

"We did. I'm working for him." Spying a large plum in the box, Torryn snatched it up and went to wash it in the sink. She took a huge bite before changing the subject. "I started cleaning out our bedroom upstairs. I'm wondering if we shouldn't do an estate sale. What do you think?"

"That might be a good idea, although I hate the thought of getting rid of Mom's possessions."

That explained why the rooms upstairs had remained untouched. "I know. Clearing out her things makes it real that she's gone. But we can each save a few things of hers that we want. I feel like Mom would want us to donate her clothes and shoes to people in need."

"I agree. I'll come over to help one day next week after work," Tess offered.

"Okay, that would be great. We'll do Mom's room together and, in the meantime, I can tackle the other areas."

"Deal."

She wiped the palm of one hand on her shorts. "Great, now that we have that settled, I'm going to throw a salad together and put a couple of chicken breasts in the air fryer for when Matthew and Connor arrive. Then I'm going to work on the brownies for Mr. Rodney. He's hired me to provide baked goods for his store."

"I don't know how you handle it all," Tess said with a chuckle. "You were always the queen of multitasking."

"I've got to make some serious money if I—" She stopped and took a breath. She almost told her sister about her need to save the house, but luckily Torryn remembered her mother's wishes not to let her siblings learn about the back taxes.

"If you what?"

"Um…nothing. Just trying to make enough to get back to my life. You know me."

"Oh, I was hoping Ryder Hill would grow on you and that you'd want to stay. I like knowing you're nearby."

Dabbing at her eyes, she said, "Oh, sis. Let's spend as much time as we can together before my time here is up. I missed you."

"I missed you, too, Tor Tor Tornado."

Torryn rolled her eyes. "Please don't call me that. I haven't destroyed Mom's garden in years." She snapped her fingers. "Speaking of garden, I'm planning to plant sunflowers with Connor. I ordered the seeds, and they should be here tomorrow."

"Oh, that sounds so nice. I remember us doing the same thing with Mom."

"Yeah, I'm carrying on the tradition. Might as well do it with Connor, since this is most likely the closest that I'm ever going to get to being a mom," she scoffed.

"Oh, my darling sister. Don't close your heart to the possibility of having a family one day."

A sudden yearning filled her, and had her wondering what it would be like to have a child of her own. But she quickly quashed that longing. She wasn't fit to be any-body's mother. Besides, what if something happened to her? There was no way she was going to chance putting a child through what she had gone through, what Connor had gone through. That little guy was definitely worm-ing his way into her heart.

"You still there, sis?" Tess asked.

"Yeah, sorry." She cleared her throat. "I was just thinking about the sunflowers and how eager Connor is to plant them," she said. "I have to decide on the perfect spot in Matthew's yard to put the seeds." She couldn't figure out where to dig in that perfectly manicured lawn of his. It seemed like even the weeds were afraid to grow there. Nothing was out of place. It was as daunting as its owner.

"Oh, that sounds so nice. As far as where to plant them, just choose good ground. Growth is guaranteed."

"You're right... That sounds like something Mom would say. But I'll take your advice. And look for good ground."

"I think that's the highest compliment you could give me. Make sure you take pictures so you have something to remember Connor by when you're gone. It sounds like you're fond of him."

"It's hard not to be. He's such a special little guy, so smart and generous."

"Sounds like you're smitten."

"Yep. For sure I am. Talk to you later." After they disconnected the call, she placed a hand over her chest, her gut twisting. A few years from now, Connor would forget her. For some reason that made her eyes tear up. Then she told herself to toughen up. Her departure was three months away and she needed to use that time to focus on saving her mother's house. Watching Connor was a means to an end. That was all.

However, whenever she saw that little face look up at her when Matthew dropped him off, she knew she was a goner. Connor had already found a place in her heart and there was no use denying it. She would embrace it for as long as she could. Maybe this was a part of the reason God had brought her here. She could give Connor the same love her mom had given to her that helped her bruised heart to mend.

Chapter Six

❧

His mind couldn't comprehend what his eyes were seeing right now. Matthew stood by the edge of the creek just before dusk the last day in May and blinked a few times, but the image was still there. He had met with his client Lucas Brennan again and the other man's stubbornness had made him weary. After work, Matthew had planned to relax with a book or watch a movie with Connor on TV, but there was nothing calming about the scene before him.

His son was covered from head to toe in mud. Caked in it. In fact, if it wasn't for those eyes, Matthew would think he was looking at someone else's kid. Come to think of it, where did Connor get that outfit? That wasn't what Connor had been wearing when he dropped off his son at Torryn's at lunchtime.

That muddy blob was running toward him, laughing, with his arms spread wide. "Dad-d-y-y!"

Matthew lifted a hand up. "Stop!" he shouted.

Connor froze in his tracks. Torryn bounced toward them holding a pair of fishing rods under her arms, and shoes in her hand, looking very pleased with herself. "Hey, we went fishing after lunch." She had mud in her hair, on her tank, and all over her shorts, plus she was barefoot.

He cringed when she drew closer. "Is that so? How did you both get all muddy?"

"Well, we were doing well until Connor slipped in the creek, and started to cry. So I encouraged him to take a swim."

"In the mud?"

"Yep. There was a small puddle by the bank. He said he couldn't swim."

"Yes, it's on my ever-expanding to-do list," he said, his eyes on her shoes. She kept swinging those shoes in her hand. He alternated between watching her and watching Connor—who had returned to the creek—and watching the shoes.

"Please tell me you didn't make him play clothes out of the curtains," he teased.

"You've seen *The Sound of Music*, I take it." She chuckled, raising her hand as if she intended to touch him. He dodged her before she made contact. "It's just dirt," she said with a smirk. "It comes off easy."

Matthew brushed at his sleeve. "That movie is one of my mother's favorites..." And Eloise's. But he kept that info to himself.

"I used my dog-walking tips from the past couple weeks and ordered some outfits for Connor online along with a pair of sneakers. They're ruined now, though." Torryn called out to Connor, who came running over. Then they marched toward his house.

Matthew couldn't let them inside his home as muddy as they were. Torryn, however, had a better idea. She headed straight to the hose in the backyard. Seconds

later, Connor was squealing and laughing as the sprin-
kler came on, dousing him with water. Of course, Torryn was right there with him, running back and forth.

For a millisecond, Matthew was tempted to join them.
It was so hot.

"Come get wet with us," Torryn called out, as if she
could read his mind.

"No, I have work to do. I'll see you when you're done
cleaning up." He headed inside. With determined steps,
he made a beeline to the linen closet to grab three oversized towels. Torryn and Connor were going to need
them, and he didn't want to risk them traipsing through
the house leaving puddles of water in their wake. Then
he decided to get a small trash bag for his son's clothes.
Once Connor had changed, he would toss them into
the wash.

A few minutes later, he heard the mudroom door
open. He handed her two of the towels before seeing to
Connor. Both of them were drenched, but she had done
a fair job of ridding them both of the dirt and mud.

"Thank you," she said, a little shyly, then used one
towel in her hair and wrapped the other around her body.

"We had fun, Daddy," Connor said, doing a jig. There
was mud in his ears, under his fingernails… Matthew
was going to put him into the bathtub right away.

"You did?" he asked absentmindedly as he slid the
wet, blackened sneakers off Connor's feet that he suspected had been white that morning.

"Yeah. It was cool." Connor jumped into his arms.

"I'm going to go get cleaned up at home," she said,
backing out the door. "I'm feeling icky and I'm pretty
sure Connor might have eaten a bug or two."

"No, I didn't," Connor said, holding his tummy. "If I ate a bug, I'd have a bellyache. Right, Daddy?"

Matthew's nose wrinkled. "Yes, I'd say you're right, buddy."

All of a sudden, Matthew didn't want Torryn to go. Connor must have felt the same because he asked, "Miss Torryn, are you coming back over?"

"I don't think so. I'll see you tomorrow."

"But I want you to read me a story."

She sought Matthew's eyes. "Fine by me, if you want," he said.

"Okay. I'll be back in a jiffy. Connor, pick out the story you want me to read." She did a two-finger wave and scurried across the lawn.

"Yay!" Connor yelled, tilting his body back in Matthew's arms.

"I'll leave the door open for you," Matthew called out.

She gave him a thumbs-up, not bothering to turn around. He watched her progress until she was safe inside the guesthouse, then he closed the door.

A warm feeling flowed through him but Matthew told himself it had nothing to do with Torryn returning. He put the baked ziti his housekeeper had prepared in the oven. Dinner would be warm and ready to go by the end of Connor's bath. In the bathroom, he stripped off the rest of his son's clothes and set them in the garbage bag. Then he put Connor in the tub and turned on the spigot.

Connor yelped and jumped back from the spray. A light red splotch appeared on his leg. In one swift motion, Matthew snatched his son out of the tub, then adjusted the water. His heart raced as he examined Connor's leg. The redness was already fading. He exhaled. "I'm sorry, son. I should have tested the water first."

"That's okay, Dad," Connor said, his eyes filling with tears. Connor patted his back. "I know it was an axdent."

Pinching Connor's cheeks, Matthew smiled. "It was an ac-ci-dent," he said, correctly enunciating each syllable. Checking the water temperature, he added some bubble bath and dumped out the toys from the mesh bag on the wall. Then he moved to place Connor inside, expecting some pushback. But his son got back into the water without a fuss.

That act of faith humbled him. No wonder God said that we had to be like children. Matthew needed to apply that principle more in his daily life.

He mulled on that principle all through Connor's story time with Torryn. Once Connor was tucked under the covers, Matthew turned on the ceiling fan and he and Torryn made their way downstairs. He asked Torryn about their fishing trip. "Did either of you catch anything?"

"No. But we're going fishing again tomorrow evening. I think I'll have to pull the rowboat out of the shed so we can go farther into the pond."

The prospect of Connor ending up in the water, drowning, terrified him. "How long do you plan on being out?"

She scratched her chin. "A couple hours at most before the sun goes down."

"I'll tag along," he said. "If that's alright with you."

"Of course. We can leave at six p.m."

"Yes, that's perfect. I'll come right after my last appointment for the day." It wasn't until she left that

Matthew recalled he needed to tell her about Blake Whitlock's call. He would be sure to rectify that the next day.

Torryn had never seen anybody fish in a suit, but Matthew didn't appear concerned that he might mess up his designer clothes. He sat on the jacket and had rolled up the bottom of his pants, but his shoes might be ruined. Yet Matthew had insisted that he didn't need to change. She suspected that he didn't have much casual wear, if any. Or maybe he just really wanted to go fishing.

He took them to his perfect spot to "catch a lot of fish." Connor gripped the side of the boat, while he kept up a steady stream of conversation, playing "I spy." She averted her gaze from Matthew's strong arms and tried to keep Connor from rocking the boat too much. It was small, so having three people inside, plus all the fishing gear, made for a tight fit.

"We're going fishing. We're going fishing," Connor yelled, dancing in the boat.

"Buddy, if you're too loud, it will scare the fish away," Matthew said.

"Yeah, we have to be really quiet," Torryn whispered.

"Okay. I can be quiet," Connor whispered, sitting down and putting a finger over his mouth. Then he stage-whispered, "How long do I have to be quiet?"

Torryn and Matthew shared a smile. Connor did a great job putting his bait on the hook of his fishing rod. Torryn not so much. Ninety minutes later, Matthew had caught three bass and Connor caught one. They took pictures before they threw them back into the water. She wasn't that fortunate. Maybe it was because she refused to use worms and used shrimp instead. The fish ate the shrimp right off her hook.

Still, they had a lot of fun. Connor had gobbled down the sandwiches and chips she had brought for him but she knew both she and Matthew were going to need to eat, too. The sun was just beginning to set and the hues of oranges and purples made for a beautiful view. Connor snuggled into her on the ride back to the dock, yawning loudly. He smelled of salt and fish. Somebody was going right into the bathtub when they got back home.

"Don't go to sleep, buddy," Matthew said. "We have to get you cleaned up and then we'll eat dinner."

"Okay," Connor said, though his head dipped to his chest and his eyelids drooped.

"I think I'll warm up our meal as soon as we get back." He raised an eyebrow. "I hope you intend to join us?"

"Yeah, I've worked up a serious appetite."

As soon as the boat docked, Matthew took his son in his arms. There was a tall, handsome man standing near the bank. He helped Matthew secure the boat before holding out a hand to her.

"I'm Blake Whitlock, owner of Whitfield Farms and your neighbor," he said with a wide smile. "I was hoping I could talk to you for a minute?"

She stiffened at his request, but said, "Um…sure."

They shook hands. Torryn looked toward Matthew, but his mouth was drawn in a thin line. He gave her a light nod. "I'll see you inside." Then he stomped toward his house, Connor's head bopping on his shoulders. If she didn't know how much Matthew valued honoring her mother's wishes, she would think he was jealous. She turned her attention onto the man standing before her.

Blake gave her a wide smile. "My orchard has been in my family for years and I would love the opportunity to expand. I've made several offers for the property but your mother didn't want to negotiate."

She had to shield her eyes with the sun still peeking over the horizon. "If my mother didn't sell to you when she was alive, what makes you think I would now that she's gone?"

"Because it would be for a good cause. This isn't about money for me. I have plans to expand the orchard, to create more business. With the extra land, I could do that, but also help others. Some of the people I hire need a place to live. I can build housing for them. It's a win-win for everyone because I plan to pay over the estimated value of the home." Blake then stated a figure that made her mouth drop.

"That's a significant amount of money."

The possibilities of what she could do with her share after splitting the proceeds with her siblings ran through her mind. She could pay off her debts and start another business. But thinking about the letter from her mom made her shake her head. That, plus the fact that if Blake was willing to pay that much, the land might be more valuable than any of her siblings had imagined.

She was about to turn him down, but Blake quickly added, "Just think about it. You're welcome to help yourself to fruit from the orchard, if you'd like. Right now, we have peaches and blueberries."

Just then, the back door opened, and Matthew came

back outside. "I will, thanks," she said, ending the conversation.

"Great. See you around." Blake strode back over to his property, whistling loudly, his confidence evident in each step. He must really think he had won her over. Still, she had to admit his offer would solve her immediate problems.

Then her cell phone beeped. It was Mr. Rodney reminding her that he was stopping by to pick up a few loaves of banana bread tomorrow about eight a.m. She sent him a thumbs-up emoji. Another message hit her phone with someone asking her to dog walk that very same morning. Again, she said yes, despite the tiredness washing over her.

Since her mother's passing, Torryn had been going nonstop. And now with three jobs, she was too busy to think of a solid plan to save the house. But what choice did she have? She walked over to Matthew, whose hands were shoved in his pockets.

"Where's Connor?"

"Poor guy was out. I ended up just cleaning him up best I could and put him straight to bed."

She nodded. "Blake wants to buy the land," she offered.

"Figures. What did he say when you told him you didn't want to sell?"

"I didn't quite decline the offer. He asked me to think about it."

Matthew splayed his hands. "What's there to think about? Your mother's instructions was very clear."

"I know," Torryn said, jutting her jaw. "But I should at least talk with my siblings and see how they feel about it."

He looked down at his feet before drawing in a deep breath. "Did Blake happen to mention that he's contesting the property line?"

"N-no." She frowned. "When did he say that?"

"When he called me the other day. I've been meaning to tell you, but didn't want to worry you until you saved your mom's property."

"That wasn't your call to keep that from me," she said, though there was no anger in her voice. So he believed she would be able to save her mom's land. Torryn only hoped that belief wasn't misplaced.

"You're correct and I apologize."

"Apology accepted." She yawned again. "Well, I'd better head on home. Got an early start with two puppies tomorrow morning. And I'm making banana bread for Mr. Rodney so I need to prep."

Matthew's eyebrows rose. "But what about dinner? We didn't eat."

"I'll throw something together at my place." With Connor asleep, it would be awkward eating alone with Matthew.

"Nonsense. I've got plenty of food here. My housekeeper made chicken parm and there's more than enough. I've got it warming in the oven right now."

"Well, if you're sure…" Torryn walked past Matthew into his home. There was nothing wrong with two people sharing a meal, right? Her dating life was nonexistent at the moment, so it was no wonder she was seeing this as more than it was. Now, if only her heart would stop beating so fast…

The smell of chicken and cheese made her stomach growl. She was glad she had agreed because her dinner would have been a meager peanut-butter-and-jelly sandwich back at the guesthouse. Matthew headed for the refrigerator. "Um, let me go wash up," she squeaked out, hating how she struggled to get the words out. A sure sign of her nervousness.

"Alright. I'll rustle us up a small salad," he said as he took out the romaine lettuce, then gave her a smile. His teeth were incredibly straight and white. The man had a smile on him for sure. She scurried to the bathroom.

As soon as she saw herself in the mirror, she gasped. Her hair was sticking up in all directions from the humidity. There was some icky stain on her face, and what was that green stuff in her teeth? She'd spoken to both Matthew and Blake looking like this?

Torryn quickly washed her face and rinsed her mouth. Then she tamed her hair somewhat. She laughed to herself. No way Matthew was going to confuse this dinner together as a date. Not looking like this.

"Why didn't you tell me my hair was a mess?" she asked as soon as she returned to the kitchen. "I stood there that whole time talking to Blake looking like the Bride of Frankenstein."

"Huh?" He squinted. "It's dark out there. I didn't notice."

She placed a hand on her hip. "Really?"

He paused chopping the cucumber to look at her. "You look just fine to me, Torryn." Something about his tone made her cheeks warm. Then he shrugged. "Besides, what does it matter what Blake thinks?" Was that a bit of frost in his voice?

"Well, you know…" She waved her hands in the air. "It was my first time meeting him. I don't want him to think I look like this all the time." She pointed to the lettuce. "You need help with anything?"

"No. No. You sit. I'm almost done."

Was he saying she looked tired? She sat on the chair at the dinette, drumming her fingers on the table.

"Do you ever stop moving?" Matthew asked.

"What do you mean?"

"You are in constant motion. At first I thought it was because you're nervous, but I don't think that's it." He came over to put the bowl of salad and a bottle of balsamic vinaigrette on the table.

"I'm not always…" She trailed off, realizing she was indeed moving. Torryn stilled.

"You have a restless energy, like you always have to be doing something." He went to take the chicken parmigiana out of the oven. It smelled amazing, which made her mouth water.

"I guess. I just like to keep busy." She jumped to her feet, and went to retrieve two plates out of the cabinet.

"I can see that, Miss Three Jobs." He gave a dry chuckle.

Her lips quirked. "My mother called me her honeybee." She grabbed plates and utensils and carried them over to the table.

His smile held admiration. "A perfect description. Bees are resourceful. A tiny but powerful part of our ecosystem. No wonder Ruth chose you to save her home."

Torryn didn't know how to respond to that. The plates landed on the table with a thud and the silverware clinked onto the plate. Matthew poured two glasses of cranberry juice, adding ice to hers. He'd noticed how she liked her drinks… *Ignore the fuzzy feels, Torryn, this is just the act of a thoughtful man.*

Matthew held out a hand and once she had taken it, he blessed their meal. Her hand felt small in his and she felt a sense of security. Like she was grounded. Which was silly. This was her neighbor. Connor's dad. Her employer.

She helped herself to a large portion of salad. Her strategy was to keep her mouth full and finish her meal quickly so she could retreat to her home. Not retreat—return. Retreat made it sound like she was running from something. And there was nothing to run from, right?

"First, feel free to use my kitchen to make the banana bread for Mr. Rodney."

"Oh, thank you."

"No problem." He jumped up and walked over to open a kitchen drawer. He came back and handed her a key. "You can let yourself in whenever."

Torryn placed a hand on her chest. "Thank you for trusting me."

He gave her a lopsided grin. "I'm already trusting you with my most prized possession—Connor. Besides, all the going back and forth between our houses proves that it makes sense to give you a key. You're right next door and if Connor needs anything…"

She nodded and placed the key in her pocket.

Then Matthew changed topics. "So let's talk about that property line," he said, cutting a piece of the chicken parm and putting it on her plate. "Ruth couldn't recall where she had placed the original land deed. If we can find it, then we can stop this dispute before it becomes a case."

She held up a finger until she finished eating a bite of chicken. "I'm in the middle of cleaning up the second-floor rooms so I'm pretty sure I'll find it. Tess is coming by to help me with Mom's room..." She suddenly felt heavy at those words. Her mother was gone. She tried to cover the sudden emotions coursing through her.

Matthew reached over to give her hand a squeeze. "Take it one day at a time. Don't push yourself to do too much too soon."

She managed a nod. "Sometimes I forget that Mom's gone and then it hits me in the chest. I have to remind myself that my mom is in a better place and that she's not in pain anymore."

"I try not to think about Eloise at all. I don't talk about her much because I don't want to get Connor upset." He cut his chicken into neat, even pieces with just the right amount of cheese and spaghetti, then popped it into his mouth. Torryn doubted he even noticed he did that.

She took a sip of her juice and dared to ask about his reasoning. "Have you considered that the opposite might be true? That not talking about her bothers Connor? Besides the one photo by his bed, you have no pictures up of his mom in the house." Torryn found that very odd.

"The first few months after she died were really hard. He used to point to her picture and cry, so I had him see a therapist who specializes in pediatric grief. But all he did was cry during the sessions. And nothing I ever said consoled him, so I put most of the photos away."

"I don't think that was the right move."

His tone changed at her frankness. "And I don't think it's your place to comment on that."

She realized she had gone too far and touched a nerve.

The air thickened between them and her appetite waned. "You're right." She picked up her plate, fork and knife and tossed them in the sink. "It's been a long day. I'd better say good night."

He jumped up. "I'm sorry. I shouldn't have come at you in such an abrupt manner. Talking about Eloise stirs up all kinds of…" He raked a hand through his hair. "It's distressing. Connor still has nightmares, calling out for his mother."

Her eyebrows rose. "Nightmares?"

"Yes." His eyes held pain and confusion. "I've tried everything—singing, praying. I've had him sleep with me. I've slept on his bedroom floor."

"Oh, Matthew." She placed a hand on his arm. "I'm so sorry. Poor little guy. What can I do to help?"

His eyes were bleak and his response made dread line her stomach. "Don't make promises you can't keep."

Chapter Seven

❧

This morning made two days in a row that Connor had slept in his own bed, nightmare-free.

Matthew, on the other hand, had tossed and turned until the wee hours of the morning, thinking about the results of the paternity test. He was still debating whether he should or should not see the test results. Last night, he had stared at the letter for a good hour before storming into his office and shoving it into the front pocket of his briefcase.

He wished he had never told his mother about Eloise's betrayal because then she wouldn't have insisted on the paternity test. Because he wasn't prepared to see the truth of Connor's parentage in front of him in black-and-white. If Connor wasn't his, then that would mean there was a man out there with potential rights to his son. Nope. It was better not to awaken that sleeping dog, or in this case, leave that letter sealed.

Besides, Connor already had a father. Him.

Getting back under the covers, he had thought about something else. Or rather, someone else. Torryn. He thought about her more and more often lately. Her hair… Her smile… The fact that she was leaving after the sum-

mer. What that would do to Connor. What that might do
to him. Pushing aside those thoughts, he picked up his
Bible and read some verses on God's faithfulness until
he fell asleep. A few hours later, he sat up in bed and
cocked his ears. Connor must not be awake yet. Their
fishing expedition the day before must have worn him
out. The only sounds he heard were the birds chirping
outside his window.

It was close to 7:00 a.m., and according to the weather
app on his phone, today was going to be a scorcher. He
had to be in his office in an hour. Rubbing his eyes, Matthew slipped out of bed and got on his knees.

Clasping his hands, he prayed. "Dear God, I am
thankful for another day. Thank You for Your faithfulness. Help me not to forget how much You have shown
Your faithfulness to me and to my son…" He cleared his
throat. "I also pray for Torryn and for Your faithfulness
toward her. Guide her on the right path as she seeks to
save Ruth's land. In Jesus's name. Amen."

Once he was dressed, the urge to sing the hymn,
"Great is Thy Faithfulness" was so strong, his lungs
loosened. He hummed a few tunes, but knowing Torryn was in the house held him back. He wasn't sure why.
Maybe it was because Connor had hyped his singing
skills. Or maybe it was because Eloise had loved his
singing. That was the song he had sung at church that
had made her approach him after the service and ask
him out for a walk in the park. Matthew smiled at the
memory. He and Eloise had enjoyed a great friendship
and prayer life while they dated. Sometimes he wondered
if they had ruined that friendship by getting married.

Because they sure did bicker. So, yeah, he swallowed

that song. Immediate guilt set in. He shouldn't allow
anything to interfere with his worship of God. He could
sing a different song. Matthew hummed a couple other
tunes before his mind returned to Torryn.

Despite his misgivings, Connor was happy, which
made him happy. She also made the most mouthwater-
ing goodies.

Today she was making banana bread. He had offered
the use of his kitchen since it was bigger than the one
in the guesthouse. Though she seemed to make a mess
while baking, the outcome was worth it. And it was good
to hear Connor laugh as he helped her.

He sniffed. Come to think of it, the house actually
smelled like banana bread. He paused. Matthew headed
down the hallway toward Connor's room.

His bed was empty. That was odd, because as soon
as he awakened, Connor bounded into Matthew's bedroom. Always. A vision of Connor going outside and
wandering around the property had Matthew frantically
running out of the room. What if his son had gotten hurt
while he'd been sleeping? Had he locked the back door
the night before? Matthew was halfway down the stairs
when he heard faint noises coming from the kitchen. He
froze. No wonder Connor hadn't come running. He was
with Torryn. Now that Matthew was sure of his son's
safety, he headed back into his room.

Once he had dressed for his work day, he went downstairs. Anticipation flooded his chest and he told himself it was because he was about to see Connor's bright
face. No other reason.

The display of baked goods on the kitchen counter
had his mouth watering. Torryn gave him a wave and a

smile as she stuffed small loaves into plastic loaf bags and then twisted bread ties around them. "I prepared an order for Mr. Rodney, but I saved enough for us." She wiped a hand on her apron, which read A Cut Above the Rest, then indicated toward the small platter with about five loaves wrapped in plastic. They were right next to the bowl of oranges, peaches, bananas and a large pineapple. He planned to cut up some fruit to take with him to work for a snack, leaving some for Connor and Torryn.

"Thanks. A man could get used to this." Why did he say that? It was a good thing his back was turned because he was afraid to see her reaction to his rash words. So he stuffed a piece of the bread in his mouth.

Connor stood on his step stool with half his body across the counter. He picked up the last piece of bread from the small plate in front of him. There were crumbs on his face and in his hair. He took a sip of orange juice and gave a hearty sigh. "It tastes yummy. Right, Daddy?"

Connor came over to hug him before tilting his head back. "Miss Torryn gave me half of a banana bread."

Ruffling his curls, Matthew asked, "Did you brush your teeth?"

Connor's hazel eyes shifted, a sign that his son had forgotten his morning routine. But Matthew didn't scold. "It's okay. You can do that when you take a bath this morning."

"Yay! Miss Torryn said I can have more if you say it's okay."

"How about a peach instead?" He pointed at the fruit basket, hoping to reduce his son's sugar intake.

"No, thanks. I like banana bread. Can I get another slice?"

"You mean the other half of the banana bread?" He placed a hand on Connor's head.

Connor jumped. "Yeah, the other one half."

He gave a nod. "Alright, but you'll have fruit the rest of the day."

"Okay, Daddy," Connor said, his eyes on the banana bread.

"Right." Connor was licking his fingers, so Matthew directed him to go wash his hands. Once they were alone, he asked Torryn, "How long have you been here?"

"Since about six-fifteen," she said. "After I took two poodles out for their morning walk."

"You did all that, then came in and baked?"

"Yep. It only took twenty minutes to walk the puppies."

She'd been up since 5:00 a.m? "How did you get the bread baked so fast?"

"I prepped last night. The only thing I had to do was drop the batter into the tins and bake them. You don't want to see the kitchen at the guesthouse right now," she said, chuckling.

"Do you need to borrow the Expedition to deliver them to Mr. Rodney?" he asked Torryn. "You can drop me off at the courthouse and I can give you a ride back when I'm done, if you don't mind waiting."

"No, he's coming by to get them. And, I uh, I actually don't have a license," she said, somewhat sheepishly.

"You don't have a driver's license?" He could hardly keep the amazement out of his voice.

She shook her head, her gaze focused on packing the

carton. "No. I…" She blew out a wisp of air. "That's why I live in cities with public transportation."

"Okay." Matthew sensed her embarrassment and figured this was a sticky subject. Gently, he asked, "Do you want to learn?"

"Um, yes. But I don't know if I'll master my fear anytime soon." Then she shrugged. "I've survived twenty-eight years without one. I suppose I'll be just fine."

"If you change your mind…" He heard the bathroom door open and the television turn on. Matthew knew that Connor was pulling up one of his favorite shows. Sure enough, he could soon hear the opening tune.

"Thanks for the offer. I will let you know." She lifted her shoulders. "The seeds came so I'm going to plant those sunflowers with Connor today."

"What time?" he asked.

"I'm thinking right before lunch." She pointed to the refrigerator, where she had posted a picture of the sunflower and a clock with the hands drawn to the time. "I made that for Connor so he can look at the kitchen clock instead of asking me."

"Smart. Are you sure you've never been a mom before?" he joked.

"Very. And I don't plan to be."

For some reason that made Matthew sad. "For what it's worth, you're doing a great job with Connor. He's so happy with you, and I can go to work without worrying about him."

Her eyes shimmered. "Thank you. That means so much to me."

Their eyes locked. And held. The air tightened. Matthew stepped toward her. Her face flushed. She really was beautiful, both inside and out. Then a loud rap on the back door made them jump. Torryn rushed to get the door and Matthew grabbed the box to hand to Mr. Rodney.

"Hey, there," he said, taking the box from Matthew.

"I know you ordered thirty but I made fifty," Torryn said. "I hope that's okay."

"That's great. I have no doubt I'll sell out again." Then there was an awkward silence.

The older man looked at Matthew and Torryn, pensive. Then he asked Matthew, "How's that case with the Brennan boy going?"

"I'm hoping we can come to a resolution today," Matthew said, not surprised that Mr. Rodney knew all the happenings in Ryder Hill. A small town held no secrets, which was why he moved from the doorway and busied himself with cutting up fruit for Connor. Mr. Rodney had a keen eye, a huge imagination and a loose tongue. And he was giving Matthew the eye as if he hadn't expected to see him in the kitchen of his own home.

"Did you bring the apples?" she asked. "I want to make an apple-cinnamon cake."

"Oo-ee, that's my favorite," Mr. Rodney said. "I haven't had good apple-cinnamon cake since before your mama got sick."

Torryn raked a hand through her hair. "Yeah, well, it's been a while since I've made it but I plan to use Mom's recipe and see how it turns out."

"Now, you make sure you save me a slice. If yours tastes even half as good as hers, I'll be placing an order for that, too, and I know quite a few people who would want cakes."

"I'll do one better and make you your own cake, plus another three for the store. So how about those apples?"

"I brought a bag of apples, like you asked. Let me put this box inside my SUV, bring in the apples and then I'll pay you your portion from yesterday's haul."

"Oh, great, thank you," she said. She wiped her hands on her apron. "Let me go check on Connor. He's been really quiet."

The last time Connor had been that quiet, he had gotten hold of a bottle of Eloise's lotion and had bathed himself with most of the contents. Connor had been two at the time, and Matthew and Eloise had laughed so hard at his antics. He was pretty sure he had it on video. Matthew made a mental note to search for the recording. Torryn would enjoy watching that.

Mr. Rodney headed to the door but Matthew intervened. "Stay here," he said to him. "I'll take out the box of banana bread and then get the apples for you."

"Alright, thanks, son." Mr. Rodney handed over the box of baked goods. Matthew went through the door, wondering how much money Torryn had earned so far from her many jobs. It couldn't be that much since she hadn't been working too long. And it would be rude to ask, wouldn't it?

But this was Torryn. So he gave it a shot.

She told him as soon as Mr. Rodney left. "I've netted eight hundred so far, including what you've paid me. Not bad, but I don't know if I'll make six grand in three months, especially since I started a payment plan with the hospital to pay my past bill from my appendix removal surgery."

"I think you will. You've got time. I plan on compensating you well for all the extra hours you've spent with Connor," Matthew said, offering.

"Not necessary," Torryn said. "Connor is a delight, and my mom wanted me to figure this out on my own. I don't think the answer is you giving me a handout." She exhaled. "I can do all things through Christ. That was one of my mother's favorite verses. The more I repeat that, the more I hope my belief will morph into reality, because right now this feels impossible."

His heart moved at the uncertainty in her tone. Matthew took her hand in his. "When Eloise died, and I realized that I was left to raise Connor on my own, I didn't think I could do it. I mean, what did I know about caring for a two year old? But my mother encouraged me, and with her help, Connor is healthy and happy. And now I will be that help to you, if you need it. All you have to do is ask."

This wasn't her first time planting in a garden, so why was she so nervous? Her heart raced and she had to constantly wipe her clammy hands on her shorts. Maybe it was because of the brave little boy marching ahead of her in Matthew's backyard who was trying to determine the perfect location for their sunflowers.

Who's going to plant flowers with me? I don't have a mom. Torryn had lost count of how many times those words had come back into her mind, touching her heart. Just then, she heard Connor as he yelled, "Is this a good spot?" He stood on the edge of the property, near a huge shrub, looking adorable in his jeans, blue T-shirt and sturdy boots.

"Hmm… How about we check out the front of the house instead of the backyard, and then we decide?"

"Okay." He skipped around the corner, and she ran after him. The sun's rays felt warm on her back and she welcomed the heat, especially since the weather had called for rain. Torryn had been relieved she hadn't needed to postpone their planting session because it was all Connor had talked about once he woke from his nap, and she would have hated to disappoint him.

The flower bed in front of Matthew's house was about six feet long, and though there were signs it had been landscaped, right now it was covered in tiny weeds. Though there was ample sunlight, there was also an awning to provide some shade. Connor hopped from one end to the other on one leg. "So, is this a good spot to plant the sunflowers?"

"Yes."

"Yay!" Connor dashed across the yards to do flips, or rather tried to do them. His poor legs couldn't fully circle, but he was determined to keep trying.

She called him over. "First we have to prepare the soil so I'm going to need your help." She shielded her eyes from the sun with her hand.

"What's soil?" he asked, bouncing over to her, his chest heaving and his forehead glistening with sweat.

"The dirt," she responded, taking out the shovel. "We have to pluck the weeds out first. So your hands are going to get dirty."

He shuddered. "Ooh. I don't want to get my hands dirty because then I can't eat."

"Sure you can. We just have to wash our hands, that's all."

"Okay, but make sure I don't forget." He mimicked washing his hands.

"I won't," she said, hiding a smile.

Torryn sat on the grass and patted the ground next to her. Connor plopped down, sitting so close that she couldn't move her arm. "Scooch over a little bit, Connor. I don't want to bop your head by accident."

He did as she asked and then patted her arm. "Bop."

She pressed his nose. "Bop. Bop."

Of course, that meant he had to do it again. "Bop. Bop. Bop." His face tilted toward hers, and he looked ready to play. If they were going to get this done, she was going to have to redirect his focus onto the garden. However, he was only four. Maybe they needed to get the wiggles out first. Or would he get too tired to work?

"Bop. Bop. Bop," he said again.

Nope. It was time to refocus. She couldn't let a four-year-old manage her, no matter how adorable he was. It was hard to say no to that cute face, so she looked away and handed him a plastic shovel. "This is yours. We have to dig up the weeds to get ready for new life." Torryn then taught him how to pull up the pesky wild-flowers. Since there was a weed barrier, they weren't that hard to pull up.

"But they look so pretty," Connor said.

"Yes, but they are pretend plants. They look real and can trick you into thinking they are good, but they can kill our sunflowers if we don't take them out. So they have to go."

"I don't want my sunflowers to die." Connor tugged even harder then. By this time, he had tossed the shovel and was using his bare hands. Torryn snapped a picture of him and texted it to Matthew.

Thank you for this. Matthew texted. I'm sorry I'm missing all the fun.

You're welcome. Connor is quite the helper. And you can help with keeping them watered.

Thank you for keeping your word.

No thanks needed. She slipped her phone in her back pocket and kept working.

When they were almost finished, Connor, his voice a mere whisper, asked, "Miss Torryn, did you know my mom died?"

"Yes, honey, you told me, remember?" She wiped at the streak of mud across his face.

"Oh, yeah. I forgot," he said, then poked out his lower lip. A few beats later, he said, "I d-didn't w-want my mommy to die."

His words hit her in the chest. "I didn't want mine to die, either."

The boy threw down the weeds in his hands, then jumped into her arms. Holding on to her, he sobbed. She hadn't expected this project to bring up painful memories for Connor or herself. This was supposed to be healing.

But then again, weren't tears a way of cleansing, of healing? There was nothing wrong with a good cry. So she allowed Connor to weep and she wept along with him, holding him tight.

"I—I m-miss her s-so m-much," he hiccupped. "D-do you m-miss y-your mom?"

Oh, this poor baby. "Yes, I do. I miss her so much my chest hurts."

He nodded like he understood, which broke her heart. "I—I c-can't talk about h-her or D-Daddy will g-get m-mad." He looked around as if he expected his father to appear, but Torryn drew him close.

Fat tears fell down her face. Her heart ached at the agony reflected in Connor's eyes. Since her hands were dirty, she couldn't wipe her face or his, so she allowed herself to ugly cry. So Connor could see that it was okay to do so.

"Daddy's not mad at you," Torryn clarified once Connor had calmed down a bit. That was important for him to know.

"Y-yes, he is. He does his face like this." Connor reared back to show his furrowed eyebrows.

She wondered if Matthew had any idea how sensitive his son was. "Maybe he's just sad." At least she hoped that was what it was. Because she couldn't think of any good reason Matthew would do that.

"Yeah...maybe..."

She wasn't sure if Connor believed her. Matthew had told her that he didn't talk about Eloise. She could now see that his doing so was a big mistake. But Matthew didn't seem like he would be receptive to advice like that.

So she answered Connor as best as she could.

"Sweetheart, you can talk about your mommy to me anytime you want. Okay?"

"Okay." He exhaled, then slumped his shoulders, like

a weight had been lifted from them. Then he sniffled. "You know what? I have a picture of my mommy in my room. Do you want to see her?"

"I would love to see a picture of your mommy," Torryn said. "Now that we've finished weeding, I am going to pour the soil, then this evening we'll plant the seeds, once it's a little cooler, if you're up to it."

Standing up, she emptied the bag of soil on the flower bed. Together, they spread the new earth around. "It's soft," Connor said. "Just like my mom."

Yes, she was going to have to talk to Matthew. Connor was eager to talk about his mother, and Matthew was stopping him from expressing himself. That wasn't healthy for a young child. Matthew had to allow Connor to go through that process. Maybe she'd talk to God about it first before approaching him. After gathering their tools, Torryn put them away in the shed, then they went back inside to wash their hands and faces.

Next, she poured them each a glass of cold water. Connor finished his in two swallows. "Now, can I show you the picture of my mom?" he asked.

"Yes, of course."

He ran up the stairs, returning barely a minute later clutching a small frame in his hands. He held it out to her. Torryn studied the beautiful woman standing next to Connor, both of them with their hazel eyes sparkling in the photo.

"My mom was pretty like you, Miss Torryn. But she wasn't a weed."

Torryn's breath caught. "No, baby. Your mother wasn't a weed at all. She was a sunflower."

"Yeah…" He lifted his chin. "I'll be right back."

Before he could dash off, she said, "Why don't you take the photo back upstairs?"

"Okay." He took it from her, holding it tenderly in both his hands. It was obvious this was a prized possession. She bit her cheek to keep from dissolving into tears again. He scampered up the steps.

"Hurry back," she yelled. "I'm going to make us a salad for lunch."

"Yum."

Torryn quickly made a chef's salad, using grilled chicken. It wasn't until she was finished putting the salad together that she realized that Connor hadn't come back downstairs and that he was super quiet. Uh-oh. Too quiet. Her stomach in knots, she took the stairs two at a time to check on him. *Lord, please let him be okay.*

But she needn't have worried. Connor was in his room, humming as he sat drawing at his kid-size desk.

"Hey, Connor, are you coming to lunch?" she asked, casually inching closer to get a look.

"Yes, I'm almost done."

With a flourish, he dropped the yellow crayon then held up his artwork for her to see. The paper was folded, so she smoothed it out and then studied his drawing of four sunflowers. His attention to detail was impressive for someone so young. "Wow, Connor, this is really, really good. I can't believe you drew this."

A smile erupted on his face. "I am the best at drawing."

"I agree." She smiled.

Connor held out his hand and she returned the paper to him. He pointed to the smallest flower. "That's me." Then he indicated the tallest, and said, "That's Daddy."

Finally, he pointed to the next one and said, "That's Mommy," and continued to the last one, and announced, "And that's you."

"Oh, thank you, baby," she choked out, bending over to give him a hug. He had included her. Wow. He had included her.

"You're welcome."

Her heart cracked open at his gesture. She couldn't tell him that she wasn't technically part of his family. But family wasn't always about blood. Looking at him, she acknowledged Connor had sledge-hammered a place in her heart.

Connor left the room talking about lunch and she trailed behind him, glancing at the sunflowers on his picture. Resolute, she dug around the junk drawer in the kitchen until she found a magnet, then she placed his artwork on the refrigerator. The first of many, she hoped. Then she stepped back, her eyes on the flowers, her heart taking in its meaning.

She kept thinking, how was she going to leave him after this summer? And more importantly, how would Matthew feel when he saw what his son had drawn?

Chapter Eight

———

Matthew stretched his back for a moment. He had been poring over documents for the past few hours. Lucas Brennan had called to say he had an emergency so they had moved their appointment to the afternoon, which was a bummer. He had been planning on going home to see how the sunflower planting was going.

His stomach started grumbling. It was close to lunchtime and he hadn't eaten yet. Pressing the intercom, he asked his assistant to order takeout. Just then, a text message came through.

Your Nana sends her love. We prayed for you. It was his mother. On the one hand, he was glad to hear from her, but deep down, he was slightly disappointed that the text hadn't been from Torryn. She had sent a photo of Connor eating lunch.

Thx. I need all the prayers I can get.

How is Connor doing? I miss him.

He's good. He misses you, too, Mom. As do I.

How are things going with you and Torryn?

That was a trick question, meant to find out if they were more than employer and employee. They were acquaintances. No, they were a step above that. Friends. Still, best to keep his responses to his mother about it impersonal.

Connor's planting sunflowers with Torryn today, he replied.

Oh, that's wonderful. Are you joining them?

No. I'm at the office.

So, at the risk of being a broken record, did you view the results?

And there it was, the true reason for her reaching out. To her credit, his mother had asked how he was doing first. His eyes fell on his open briefcase. Then he frowned. The letter wasn't there. Matthew got up to search through the pockets of his bag, all the while trying to replay his steps. Heart pounding, he ran out to the parking lot to see if it had fallen on the pavement. The last thing he wanted was for someone to open the letter and see the paternity results. This was a small town and that would bring up a lot of questions. He certainly didn't want his son to face any kind of speculation. He unlocked his car to check inside.

Nothing.

Where on earth could it be? He rubbed his jaw and looked upward. If he had opened the envelope when it first arrived, this wouldn't be happening. Or he could have just left it on his nightstand. If asked, he would be hard-pressed to find an answer to why he had put it in his briefcase in the first place. Glancing at his watch, he groaned. Lucas Brennan was due to arrive in minutes and he still hadn't eaten. He would have to search for it later.

Matthew made his way inside, his heart pinched at losing something so personal.

That was all he thought about while he scarfed down his salad.

And it was on his mind when Lucas came in with his wife, Paige. While they pored over Lucas's mother's paperwork, Matthew retraced his steps in his mind. But then Lucas said something that snapped his attention back to his clients.

Lucas slipped Paige's hand in his. "We believe my mother wasn't of sound mind to make such a decision, so we're contesting her will."

"Are you sure that's the path you want to take?" Matthew asked, his voice a bit steely. "You could be looking at years before you see a dollar, and these cases have a tendency to drain your funds."

Lucas shifted in his seat, cleared his throat and mopped his brow.

Paige gripped her husband's hand, her knuckles white. "We received Agatha's medical records and we believe she had an underlying mental-health condition that impaired her decision-making."

"I have her signed testament that she *was* in her right mind and a psychiatrist signed off on it." Matthew leaned forward. "Your mother left you a significant sum. But she also wanted to use her wealth to help others."

"She wasn't thinking about her grandchildren. The twins deserve to go to the best colleges," Paige snapped.

He worried this would become confrontational if he didn't shift gears. "Everyone who knew Agatha knew how much she loved her granddaughters and vice versa. Are you prepared for them to know about her illness? They're fourteen and you won't be able to shield them from learning that if you go to court."

Lucas's eyes widened. He faced his wife. "I do have a good job, you know. Our daughters will be well taken care of."

She clutched her neck. "I... I'm not saying you're not a good provider for us, but this money should be yours. Your mother had no right to deny you your full inheritance."

"My mother loved helping people and it was her money. She earned every penny and she saved and invested it all. Who are we to dictate what she does with it?" Lucas said.

Matthew sat back in his chair. Lucas defending his mother's actions was more than he had hoped for.

Paige's mouth twisted. "Why are you changing your mind now that we're here? You weren't saying this to me at home. It's Matthew's job to say whatever he has to so you give in. He represents your mother's estate." She folded her arms and glared at Matthew.

He was about to object to her accusation when Lucas piped up.

"Did you not hear Matthew say that it could take years to go through the proper channels? Years, Paige. Not months." He splayed his hands. "Do you think I want to have my name plastered in the town paper and chance the girls reading about me going against my mother's wishes?" His tone gentled. "How do you think they would feel if they read about their grandmother's diagnosis?" He shook his head. "I don't want to hurt Natalia and Natashia. And I won't tarnish my mother's reputation."

Paige's shoulders deflated. "I hadn't thought about them." Tears welled and she looked at Matthew with shame and apology in her eyes. "I only wanted the best for my daughters." She took Lucas's hand in hers. "And my husband."

Matthew nodded. "I understand. But sometimes doing the best for your family means leaving things as they are."

Lucas nodded. "Sound advice."

Clearing his throat, Matthew broached the delicate matter of what to do with Agatha's home, which was so large it could be considered a mansion.

"We were planning on selling it," Lucas said. "Mom had so much stuff, I want to go through everything but I honestly have no idea where to even begin."

"I'm on call for the next few weeks or I would do it," Paige said. She was one of the town's few pediatricians.

"I think I might know someone," Matthew said. "She's a home organizer and I'm sure she would be willing to do it."

"Does she offer weekend hours?" Lucas asked. "And is she available a few weeks in July?"

"Let me find out," he said, although he was pretty confident in Torryn's response. He fired off a text. Are you available to help organize an estate?

When?

Evenings and weekends. Starting in July for a few weeks.

Sure. As long as I'm not needed to watch Connor...
Thanks for the rec.

He passed on her contact information to Lucas and
Paige. When they left his office, Matthew leaned back
in his chair and smiled. *Thank You, God.* He couldn't
have asked for a better outcome, plus he had secured Torryn with another way to earn money, which he felt good
about. Matthew really admired Torryn's work ethic. She
was skilled with multitasking and still managed to make
time to babysit Connor.

She had all these fun things planned for her and Connor, and Matthew found himself not wanting to be left
out. Pulling up his calendar, Matthew cleared some time
off his schedule.

His cell dinged. His mother had texted a question
mark. Apparently, he had forgotten to answer her question about whether or not he had read the results.

Sorry, Mom. I was with clients. No, I didn't open it.

Why not?

There was no way he was telling his mother that he
had lost the letter with the results. So he said, It's not
the right time.

Ugh. Rip off the Band-Aid already.

I promise I will let you know when I do it. Please don't
ask again, Mom.

As you wish.

On his drive home that afternoon, his words to Lucas came back to him. *Sometimes doing the best for your family means leaving things as they are.* But was this true in his case? Was he doing better for Connor by not finding out the results? He wasn't so sure…

"You've got a serious tan, but it suits you," Tess said, observing. Her sister had popped over just as Torryn had finished icing the batch of apple-cinnamon cakes she had baked. Unlike Torryn, who was dressed in a bright yellow top and brown shorts, Tess wore black dress slacks and a black-and-white striped blouse.

"Thank you. Connor and I were outside this morning tilling the earth, and we just finished planting and watering the sunflowers seeds. Just like we used to do with Mom."

While Connor played on the trampoline in the backyard, the sisters sat on the back porch under the shade to catch up. Torryn had given her sister a slice of the cake with some fresh-squeezed lemonade that the housekeeper had made. She had only seen Anna in passing, but Torryn had left a note on the fridge complimenting her on the right blend of tartness and sweetness.

Connor came over, his body dripping with sweat, to gulp some water from his water bottle and give her a hug. Since their talk that morning, he had been a little clingy, but she didn't mind because she was feeling the same. Losing a mother at any age was tough, but it was a whole other thing when a child had to grapple with the concept that Mommy isn't coming back. Ever.

After giving her another quick embrace, Connor went back to the trampoline.

"Aw, how sweet," Tess said, touching her abdomen, her voice winsome.

Torryn glanced at her sister. "Do you ever think of him?" she asked softly, referring to the infant that Tess had been forced to give up for her adoption as a teen. Since Torryn was eight years younger, she hadn't understood much of what had happened, but she knew Tess and her mom had been feuding for months. Tess had even threatened to run away, but in time, Tess and her mom had mended fences.

She'd expected Tess to evade the question, as usual, and change the subject. But to her surprise, her sister whispered, "I try not to… But I do. All the time." She brushed a wayward curl away from her face. "He'll be eighteen next month." Her voice hitched. "Maybe that's why I've been thinking about him so much lately. I was close to his age when I gave birth."

She didn't know what to say to comfort her sister, so she reached over to take her hand and gave it a squeeze. She remembered Tess crying for weeks, isolating herself from everyone, including her best friend—former best friend—Justin Washington. That summer had been the end of her carefree, rebellious youth. Torryn's heart ached.

"Do you think you'll have more children one day?" Torryn asked.

Her sister gasped, her hand covering her mouth. "Didn't I ever tell you? I—I can't. Complications of childbirth." She broke eye contact to wipe the tears welling in her eyes.

Her gut wrenched at the anguish in Tess's admission. "Oh, sis. I'm sorry. I didn't know. I didn't know."

"It's alright. I didn't tell anyone." Tess kept her gaze straight. "I was sixteen when I got pregnant and seventeen when I gave birth. It was a rough delivery. I only learned of the complications a couple years later. At the time, I was so angry at Mom, and God." She wrapped her arms around herself. "I saw it as God punishing me for acting out after our biological mom's death." Her chin wobbled. "I gave my son away and I'll never have another."

"You don't have to have a natural birth to be a mother. Ruth Emerson was the perfect example of that."

Tess took a swig of the lemonade and drew in a deep breath. "Never mind. It's all in the past and I didn't come here for that. Let's talk about something else."

Torryn felt compelled to respond. "God doesn't work that way, sis. He is love and it excludes no one. I know you know that."

"Yeah," she snorted. "He has a funny way of showing it, I guess."

"Can we pray together before you leave?"

Instead of answering, Tess took a bite of the cake. She closed her eyes and moaned. "Oh, my, this is amazing. It's almost as good as Mom's. Every time I had a slice of her apple-cinnamon cake, it made the day brighter. More hopeful."

Torryn ate some of her cake. "Oh, you're right, Tess." She smiled. "I think I just aced Mom's recipe. Mr. Rodney is coming by tomorrow morning to pick up two cakes. One of them he's going to sell in the store by the slice. It's a trial."

"Look at me, Miss Torryn," Connor yelled, doing backflips on the trampoline. "Look at me."

Tess stood and clapped her hands. "Yay, you're doing it!"

"I see you," she shouted, her fists in the air. "Do your

thing, Connor." She didn't know how he still had so much energy to keep jumping but he was steady bouncing up and down. "You have five more minutes and then we're going inside. Okay?"

"Okay!" he yelled, pumping up his speed.

Tess cocked her head at Torryn. "You would make a great mother."

Ignoring that not-so-subtle hint, she scoffed at her sister. "No, no. That's not for me. Love brings nothing but loss." She kept her eyes on Connor, who had slowed to a small bounce.

"God is love," Tess said, throwing her words back at her. "Are you saying loving Him brings loss?" She pointed upward, to the sky.

"No, I'm not saying that. His love gives me strength. It's solid. Everlasting. I can love Him without fear. But I was in that car when Mom crashed…" She shuddered. "One minute, we were talking and laughing and the next…she was gone and our whole world changed." With a start, she realized how losing their biological mother at a young age had had a tremendous effect on them. It had manifested in their lives in different ways.

"It sure did." The sisters hugged. Then Tess laughed. "We are going to have to shake off the doldrums or we won't be able to sort through Mom's things without falling apart."

"Oh, we're going to fall apart, but we have each other's backs." She gave her sister another hug. "We'll bear each other's burdens until we get to the end."

"Yes, we will. Together."

She called out to Connor, who was now sitting on the

trampoline. His face was flushed with heat. "We're getting ready to go inside, Connor. Come get some water."

"Alright..." He shimmied off the trampoline and charged toward her, slamming into her midriff. "I love you, Miss Torryn."

"I love you, too, Connor," she returned. Handing Connor his water bottle, she tossed her sister a look and said, "Yes, I know I'm eating my words from a few minutes ago, but it's impossible to keep him at arm's length. Every day I'm with him, he does something that trips up my heart." After directing Connor to get his shoes from the edge of the trampoline and put them on, she then told her sister about Connor's drawing and what it represented.

"Wow." Tess sniffled. "I don't know how you're going to resist him 'cause he's wrapping his way around my heart and it's barely been thirty minutes since I got here."

"I know."

"Does that struggle expand to his father?" Tess raised her eyebrows. "Matthew Lawson is one attractive man."

"Is he?" Her voice squeaked. "I hadn't noticed. I don't pay attention to what he looks like." However, if she had to, she could describe what Matthew had worn to work, from his shirt to his shoes. But she was an organizer and had trained herself to look at details. At least that's what she told herself.

"Really?" Her sister placed a hand on her hip. "You expect me to believe that?"

Coming over, Connor rubbed his tummy and burped. "Are we going to eat cake for dinner?" he asked.

"No, you're having leftovers, baby."

He tilted his head. "You're not eating with us?"

"I don't know..." She straightened. She had to keep herself emotionally distant as best she could, despite the havoc he was wreaking on her heart. "I have a lot to do so I think it will be just you and Daddy tonight."

His head lowered and he pouted. "Okay, but I'll miss you. Daddy will miss you, too." For some reason those words caused her heart to flutter.

"I don't think you're going to win this battle," Tess said. "Makes me wonder if Connor is the only one you're getting attached to."

"We're...friendly. Friends. Yeah, just friends."

Tess picked up her purse. "I'm going to head up to the main house and get started. See you over there."

"We'll be right behind you."

"I'll race you back to the house to wash our hands, Connor. On your mark... Get set..."

"Go!" Connor boomed, dashing off toward his house.

Head down, she chased after him, picking up speed before she crashed into a hard chest. Tripping over her feet, she would have fallen if strong hands hadn't steadied her.

"I was coming to get Connor so we could check out the flower bed, but it seems as if I have caught my very own sunflower," Matthew teased. Looking into his eyes, her heart skipped a beat, and her mouth went dry.

His eyes locked with hers.

Then she heard Connor shout, "Miss Torryn, why are you hugging my Daddy?"

Chapter Nine

There was no missing it. The drawing on the refrigerator door, held up by a tiny magnet. It was the only thing on the stainless-steel fridge.

It was the first thing Matthew saw after he entered the house. He had been staring at it for the past ten minutes, while Connor sat in the living room watching an episode of *Peppa Pig*. He should be getting Connor's bath ready, but he couldn't tear his gaze away from the drawing.

Connor had been extremely clear about whom each of the sunflowers represented. Knowing his son, he was pretty sure that Connor had explained his picture to Torryn as well.

Oh, boy, and not even thirty minutes ago, Matthew had called Torryn his sunflower.

He hadn't known the significance at the time, but his words—uttered in jest—now had a deeper meaning. And surprisingly, he was alright with that. Not that he intended to do anything about it, but it was nice to know he could be interested in another woman.

Albeit one who would remain a friend.

Because if they became more than friends and things didn't work out, it would break Connor's heart if she didn't come around anymore. So, for his son's sake, he would content himself by solidifying their friendship. There were many times since Eloise's passing that he'd wondered what would have happened if they had remained friends instead of marrying.

As friends, they had shared much laughter and sung together, but as spouses, they had argued more than they had smiled and, somewhere in the midst of all that hurt, he had lost himself. He hadn't worshipped through song in months. He read, he prayed, he hummed, but he hadn't sung.

Every time he opened his mouth, he thought of how he had been at church in worship, singing the hymn, "Great is Thy Faithfulness," while Eloise had been cheating on him. The appalling irony. Her infidelity had left him with…doubts. Not about Connor. But about himself. His ability to keep a woman's interest from waning once the honeymoon phase was over. Eloise had told him she had grown bored with him, with his practical nature, and her honesty had crushed him.

Immensely.

They had sought couples counseling, and their relationship had ended stronger than when it had begun. But the thought of potentially facing a similar rejection with Torryn stopped him from going any further in their relationship.

But her sparkling eyes made him smile.

Then he remembered that he needed to continue searching for the letter. While Connor was occupied with the TV show, he checked every corner of the kitchen, including the trash. Then he checked the living and dining rooms but it wasn't to be found.

After making his way to his office, Matthew picked through every corner of the room.

Nothing.

His insides started to knot. What if Torryn had found the letter and opened it? What if she knew the questions surrounding Connor's birth and decided to tell her sister, who then told someone else, and then the gossip would spread through the town? He shuddered to think about it.

After checking to see Connor was still into his show, Matthew dashed up the stairs into his bedroom, pulled out his nightstand drawer and tossed the contents on his bed.

"Daddy, are you upstairs?" Connor called out.

"Yes, come into my room."

Connor came and jumped onto his bed right in the middle of the papers. "You've made a mess, Daddy."

"Yes, but I'm looking for something."

"What are you looking for?"

Matthew looked into those hazel eyes and paused. What a question. What was he looking for when he already knew the answer? Connor was his son. "I'm not looking for anything worth mentioning."

"Okay. Am I going to have my bath now?"

"Yes. Let's get you all cleaned up and then we can go eat."

"I miss Miss Torryn," Connor said, scooching to the edge of the bed. Matthew gathered up everything, stuffed it back into the drawer and slipped it back into the nightstand. Then, after taking his son's hand, Matthew and Connor went to the bathroom, where he started up the bathwater and poured in a generous amount of bubble bath.

Soon, lots of foamy bubbles appeared in the tub. He

put Connor inside and then dropped in the toys. Connor dipped his head into the soap and when he resurfaced, the bubbles framed his face like a wig, a beard and a moustache.

Quickly pulling out his phone, Matthew snapped a photo and sent it to Torryn.

Torryn's response was OMGosh!! He is the cutest old man I ever saw.

LOL. I figured you would get a kick out of that.

Matthew placed a heart emoji response on her last text and turned his attention back to his son.

Thirty minutes later, he was taking their meat loaf dinner out of the oven when Connor began pouting. "I wish we were having dinner with Miss Torryn."

"Me, too." Without her here, the house seemed quiet. He missed her energy, her presence. He felt genuine enjoyment when he was around her.

"Can we go, Daddy? Can we go to Miss Torryn?"

Spontaneously, he said, "Yes. Let's pack up our dinner and our cake and head over." If she asked why they had come over without an invite, he could truthfully say Connor wanted to share a meal with her. And he was pretty sure that if he didn't go over with food, Torryn would end up munching on popcorn for dinner. So, really, he was being altruistic. Before he could change his mind, he and Connor gathered the food and headed out the door.

"What did you say when Connor asked why you were all hugged up on his father?" Tess giggled, as she folded, then placed the last of Ruth's dresses in the bin designated for donation. The local thrift shop would be by before the week was out to pick up the bins.

"I didn't say anything. I distracted Connor with tummy tickles then I got out of there." Torryn laughed. Sitting on the edge of her mother's bed, she sorted through all the letters and magazines that her mother had placed in boxes. The chore didn't feel as daunting with her sister by her side. Then she admitted, "For a second, I felt like Matthew was going to kiss me. So I was glad for Connor's interruption."

Her cell buzzed with a text from Matthew and her heart began to pound. He had sent an adorable picture of Connor in the bathtub.

She quickly responded by placing a heart on the picture, tamping down her twinge of disappointment that Matthew hadn't been as affected by those few moments as she had been.

Her cell buzzed again. This time it was another potential dog-walking client using the online scheduler Torryn had placed on the free website she had created to track her numerous tasks. It wasn't the best but it was functional, just like the free version of an online billing system she used. She had already blocked off the three weekends that the Brennans had requested for their mother's estate clearance. She had to create an invoice for her services but figured she would confer to Matthew about a reasonable rate.

Once she had confirmed her time for the next morning, Torryn noticed her sister had gone silent. She looked over to the corner where Tess was standing, holding a photo in her hand, tears running down her face.

"What's wrong, sis?" She put down the papers, then ambled over to touch her sister's arm.

"I didn't know Mom had this. I don't even know when she took it." Tess waved the photo before drawing it close to her chest. "But I can't believe she's had this all these years. I found it in the folds of one of Mom's jackets."

"Let me have a look."

Tess handed over the photo, then covered her face while she sobbed. It was a picture of a teenage Tess standing in the kitchen by herself, hugging her rounded abdomen. Tess's eyes were closed and she had a wide smile on her face. "Wow."

"I wanted him. Oh, how I wanted my child." Tess sniffled.

Then she wiped her face with the back of her hand. "I don't remember taking many pictures when I was pregnant."

"Was this the only one?"

"I'm not sure."

Torryn went over to pick up her mother's jacket, which Tess must have dropped to the floor. There were two more photographs. One with the three of them, with Torryn standing in the middle smiling. Tess had her head dipped low, her eyes peering up from under her bangs and her hands touching her baby bump.

"I think I remember this day. We had gone fruit picking in the orchard next door. That must have been before the Whitlocks purchased it."

Tess came to where she stood. "Yes, it used to be our playground. A good spot to play hide-and-seek plus stuff our tummies. I can't tell how many times Mom scolded us for ruining our appetites eating all those oranges."

They shared a small laugh.

"It's where I went when I needed air. I used to climb this big tree trunk but as my pregnancy progressed, I would nestle under the huge tree and read."

"That orchard was my runaway spot." Torryn shook her head. "Remember how I used to run away all the time?"

"Yes. I used to pretend to cry when you left. But I knew all your hiding places, including the attic."

Her eyes went wide. "You knew where I was?"

"Yes, but as long as we knew you were safe, Mom and I let you have your time alone. We knew you'd be back in time for dinner."

"I think I'll take Connor fruit picking tomorrow. He'll enjoy that." She scrunched her nose. "I'll have to remember to take lots of pictures."

Tess cocked her head. "You don't have to leave, you know. Ryder Hill is your home. The guesthouse is big enough for you and Nigel. And Nigel told me he's going to get started on the roof of the main house as soon as he moves in so you'd have the guesthouse to yourself once it's finished. Although, by the sound of things, it might be both Nigel and Lisa moving in."

"Oh, wow. Their marriage is really happening, then?"

"It appears that way."

Letting that sink in for a moment, Torryn said, "I'm enjoying being closer to you, and I love that we're spending time together. Even in death, Mom unites us." And Connor and Matthew were right next door. That was very appealing, especially since a small kernel of attraction was forming on her end. One that was both unintended and a wee bit scary. But Matthew might not feel the same about her.

"Why is it so hard for you to open up to the possibility of a relationship?" her sister asked.

"I don't want to be hurt again if I can help it. Not that I know for sure that Matthew is interested." Yet there had been a definite curiosity in the depths of those gray irises of his. A question of *what if.*

"I get that, but you might be missing out." Her sister went over to the window that overlooked the Lawson property. "And there's a sweet little boy that needs a mother's love."

At those words, her heart melted. "Oh, sis. You're not playing fair."

"I agree I have selfish motives."

"If I stayed here, I'd have to learn to drive. I have my permit, but I only use it as a form of ID. That's it."

Tess patted her back. "We can't let our past and our fears hold us back because if we do, are we truly living? As long as we're breathing, we have an opportunity for a do-over. That's why I plan to open a home for teenage mothers with my portion of the money. I want these girls to have the chance to raise their child."

"Oh, sis. That is a phenomenal idea." But it wouldn't come to fruition if she didn't save her mother's property first. The pressure wrapped around her. She needed to earn more money. Fast.

"Thanks. And you have the power to impact lives, too, you know. Just put yourself out there." She touched Torryn's cheek. "At least admit that you *like* Matthew."

"I do like him. He's honest and hardworking and I

can see the big love he has for Connor, though I don't agree with how he shows it."

It was getting late, so after closing up the main house, the sisters walked across the grass to the guesthouse, but not before Torryn grabbed a bag of toys for Connor. "Do you want to come over to my place? I can throw something together for us to eat." Just as Tess asked the question, the doorbell rang.

The sisters made their way downstairs. When Torryn opened the door, Matthew and Connor stood there holding plastic storage containers and whatever was in there was smelling pretty good. Her tummy grumbled.

Connor suddenly said, "Ro-o-ar-r-r-r." Then he nudged his father's leg. "See, Daddy. I told you that Miss Torryn was hungry."

"We have meat loaf, mashed potatoes and veggies. Way too much food," Matthew said, trying to explain but looking sheepish—and adorable.

A flush of excitement filled Torryn. "Well, you've come to the right place, neighbor. We're more than happy to help you eat." She stepped back and let them inside the guesthouse. They headed toward the dinette in the kitchen.

Connor mimicked the waddle of a duck. "Quack. Quack." The chair scraped as Connor climbed onto it.

"You know what? I forgot that I had this thing to do," Tess said, grabbing her handbag and making her way to the front door. "I'll catch up with you later, sis." She gave a two-finger wave. "Have fun, you guys."

Torryn rolled her eyes, her cheeks warm. Her sister was as subtle as a truck rumbling down a highway. Once the door locked behind her, Torryn went over to Matthew, who was putting out the food on the table. "Sorry about my sister's obvious attempt at matchmaking." She went to get a couple of plates and a plastic bowl for Connor.

"Matchmaking?"

Did he not see things that way? She had better change the subject fast. "I'm taking Connor blueberry picking tomorrow afternoon. I figure we'll cut through to the orchard since Blake said we could go anytime."

"Of course, he would," Matthew said, sounding peeved. Jealous, maybe?

Hiding a smile, she swung around to lock eyes with him, but he was focused on serving Connor a small portion of vegetables along with a slice of meat loaf and a small scoop of potatoes. "I don't like carrots," Connor said, moving his fingers on the table like they were piano keys. She'd forgotten that Matthew played piano.

"Are you giving Connor piano lessons?" she asked.

His head popped up. "What? Um, no. I haven't played in a while." He directed Connor to say grace, all the while avoiding eye contact. She frowned. Why was Matthew acting all nervous? He was making her jittery.

She placed a hand on his arm. "Is everything alright?" she asked, desperate to break the tension between them. "Do you not want me taking Connor onto Blake's property?"

"No, I'm fine. In fact, why don't I join you on your excursion?"

"Of course," she said. "Connor would love it."

"Great," he said, rubbing his chin. "Forgive me if I seem off. I'm just distracted. I lost an important piece of mail today and I've been searching for it since I got home."

Her shoulders relaxed. She moved to sit, thanking him when he held out her chair for her. "What kind of mail is it?" she asked,

"It's, uh, personal."

"Oh, I didn't mean to pry. Only to help."

"I know." He smiled. "The contents of this letter are… life-changing. I would hate it if it fell into the wrong hands." Her curiosity piqued, but Matthew didn't elaborate further. He dug into his meal and changed the topic. "I want to revisit the idea of teaching you to drive. It would make things easier with all your jobs and we could stay on the back roads until you felt comfortable enough to go on the main road."

Tess's words about not letting her fears hold her back prompted her to give his offer serious consideration. The endearing expression on Matthew's face, along with the idea of spending time with him, led her to agree. "Okay, I'll try. But I warn you that I'm a terrible student. Even my driving instructor gave up on me." She tapped her feet on the wood. "I'm already nervous just thinking about it."

"Not to worry. I'm patient." He gave her hand a squeeze. "You're in good hands. You'll see. My schedule is open tomorrow so we can go after your dog walking tomorrow and before your venture into the orchard with Connor."

She nodded, her heart hammering in her chest. That had nothing to do with getting behind the wheel and everything to do with the man who would be sitting next to her in the passenger seat.

Chapter Ten

❧

Driving with Torryn was nothing like he had imagined. It was much much worse. For one thing, she was
too busy rambling on about her cakes when she needed
to keep her hands on the wheel and her eyes on the road.
When she wasn't chattering, she had her foot heavy on
the gas. Matthew had lost count of how many times he
had told her to brake.

She was quick to obey, but when she did, it was a slam
and not a gentle press. Matthew had to keep clutching the
visor to stop from banging his head. If this continued, he
was going to get a whiplash. The only person who found
it all exhilarating was Connor. Every time she braked,
his son would raise his hands and shout with glee.

Matthew checked on Connor, ensuring himself for
what had to be the tenth time that his son was securely
strapped into his car seat. When they started out, she
had clutched the steering wheel tight, barely inching
forward. Then he had encouraged her to go faster since
they were on the back roads and she had accelerated to
close to seventy miles an hour. Torryn approached her
driving like she did her life—it was all or nothing. He

was going to show her how to be content driving at medium speed, or at least heed the road signs.

She jammed on the brakes.

Wiping his brow, he asked Torryn to put the car in Park. "I saw a squirrel and I didn't want to hit him," she said, her eyes fixed on the gravel in front of her.

"That squirrel was a good fifty feet away."

"I told you I was no good at this." She grabbed the door handle and was ready to jump out of the car.

But he placed a hand on her arm to stop her, and squared his shoulders. "Let's go again."

"Why are you trying to help me?" she asked, gritting out the words, her frustration evident. "I'm never going to be at ease behind the wheel."

Taking her hand, Matthew waited until she faced him to give her a piercing gaze. In her eyes, he saw fear and disappointment. A part of her wanted to do this or she wouldn't have gotten a permit. "I understand that you're petrified but you have to control the car. You can't allow this vehicle to control you."

"That's some pretty good advice. It's just…" She released a breath of air. "Every time I'm behind the wheel, I flash back to my biological mother driving for the last time. She misjudged the turn at an intersection, and in an instant, she was gone."

"I'm sorry. I had no idea," Matthew said. "How old were you?"

"I was six."

"Only a couple of years older than Connor." He looked back at his son. Connor was blessed that he still had Matthew to raise him. He hadn't heard Torryn mention a father, so he assumed that that man hadn't been involved in their lives.

"Listen, here's what I think is holding you back. You're focused on what could go wrong when you're behind the wheel. What I want you to think about when you press that gas are the good things that come from driving a car."

She gave him the side-eye. "How is that supposed to help?"

"It can't hurt to try, right?" he countered.

She shrugged. "You're right, it can't." Then she put her hand on the gear.

He placed his hand over hers. She stiffened under his touch but then he felt her muscles ease under his palm. "Let's go to the fork in the road. Now, before you put the car in gear, I want you to take deep breaths, close your eyes and visualize driving to the end of the path."

She looked skeptical, but did as he suggested. Matthew whispered a prayer. When she opened her eyes, he said, "Now, I need you to say 'I am going to drive to the fork in the road and back and I will be just fine.'"

Squaring her shoulders, Torryn repeated his words twice. The second time around she sounded hopeful, almost like she believed him. "Alright. Now, let's go."

She drove close to the curb, moving at about twenty miles per hour, and sweat lined her forehead, but Torryn made it to the fork in the road and back to his house. Matthew pumped his fist in the air. "You did it! You drove, Torryn! We can practice again tomorrow."

Connor mimicked him. "You did it, Miss Torryn!"

Torryn jumped out of the vehicle, bent over and placed her hands on her thighs. Once Matthew and Connor had exited, she said, "My legs were wobbly the entire way and I was scared I'd press the brake instead of the gas." She exhaled, then straightened, her eyes warm. "Thank you. Thank you for helping me. For the first time in years, I feel as if I really could learn to drive." She walked over to him and embraced him. He detected the slight scents of peach and vanilla from her hair.

Matthew hugged her back. It had been a long time since he had hugged a woman and he had to admit, it was as good as he'd remembered. He felt a tiny hand snake between them. "I want to hug Miss Torryn, too, Daddy."

Laughing, Matthew and Torryn stepped back to give Connor access. Then they all hugged each other. After a few beats, he stepped back and asked how things had gone with the cakes she had made for Mr. Rodney the day before.

"He called me last night and told me that he wanted to hire me as a supplier for his store full-time. In fact, he extended a very generous offer."

"That's exciting," he said. "Maybe now you only need to work one job instead of many."

She bit her lower lip. "I told him I would think about it. In the meantime, I offered to make five more cakes."

"Why do you need time to think about it?" The question had torn out of him before he could stop himself. "Sorry, but I want to chime in here, as a friend. That job is a chance at stability." His eyebrows rose as realization dawned. "Oh, you don't want to do anything that offers that level of stability, do you? Especially since you'll be leaving in a few months. Is that it?" He drew Connor close to him.

"I—" She twisted her shirt in her hands. "I can't have anyone depend on me like that."

"Why not?" he asked, trying to convince himself that his gut was churning at the thought of her impending departure purely because of her help with Connor. Nothing more.

"My life is in Philly." She stepped away from him and Connor and walked toward his house. "Besides, once I pay my mother's taxes, I have no real solid reason to stay." She pinned her gaze on his.

Matthew remained silent, swallowing his protest. He couldn't offer her more than friendship. At least, that was what he kept telling himself, ignoring the tightening in his chest.

As soon as they entered the kitchen and washed up, Torryn put him to work chopping apples. "I want to get the batter prepped before we go fruit picking."

Connor sat in a chair in the kitchen watching them, but after he gave a huge yawn, Matthew decided to move his son to lie down on the couch. He placed Connor there, smiling as his son sighed and fell asleep almost immediately. He took a moment to study how peaceful his child was in repose, then smoothed Connor's hair. As he moved to stand, he heard a crinkle. His brow furrowed as he leaned forward to investigate. There was a piece of paper sticking up between the seat cushions. Matthew fished out an envelope. Turning it over, he stilled when he recognized the return address.

This had come from the place that had done his paternity tests. However, the envelope had been opened. Judging by the tiny rips around the edges, Matthew figured Connor had done the deed. But where was the actual letter? Moving Connor to another couch, he dug around and lifted the seat cushions but there was nothing but crumbs.

Walking into the kitchen, he held up the envelope for Torryn to see. "I found this stuffed between the seat cushions. Connor got a hold of it." He watched her keenly.

Torryn spared him a brief glance, her attention focused on sifting flour. "I'm so glad you found what you were looking for."

"I didn't," he said. "It's empty." He opened the envelope to emphasize his point.

"I'm sorry but I haven't seen it." She rested her hands on the counter and stared at him. "What's in it?" she asked.

"I don't want to burden you with my problems, Torryn."

She tapped her shoulders. "Try me. I'm stronger than I look."

Matthew released a heavy sigh. "It was results of a paternity test. I needed to know if Connor was my biological child."

Later that afternoon, Torryn lagged behind Matthew and Connor, who was sitting on his father's shoulders, as they walked through the orchard. Matthew had changed into a crisp white T-shirt, a brand-new pair of jeans and black sneakers. She snuck a picture of him with his son donned in similar clothing. Okay, she might have taken more than one. Her plan was to print a few copies to put in Connor's bedroom.

Connor bounced as he pointed out the different kinds of fruit trees. Since there were only three other families within earshot, she and Matthew didn't try to curtail his enthusiasm. Besides, Connor's chatter was the perfect cover while she tried to process Matthew's information. She had so many questions but, once he had dropped his bombshell, he'd refused to go into more detail. She adjusted a tote strap she had bought to store their blueberries and other fruit.

Waving at her, Connor called out, "Hello, Miss Torryn. I picked some peaches. And guess what? Guess what? Daddy said I could eat some!"

She hurried over to see. "Oh, wow, Connor, that is amazing and I think your daddy is right because this smells tantalizing." Her eyes met Matthew's and a warm, fuzzy feeling came over her. He gave her a peach, their fingers touching for an instant.

Just then, the sound of hooves drew her attention to a man on horseback heading in their direction. Rubbing her arms, she recognized Blake Whitlock. He was dressed in a plaid shirt, jeans and a cowboy hat, looking every bit the cowboy.

"Yeehaw!" Connor said as his father slipped him off his shoulders and into his arms.

"Hello, little man," Blake greeted, giving Connor a lopsided grin. Then he peered over at her. "I heard you were here so I had to pop over to welcome you to Whitlock Farms." Then he tipped his hat toward Matthew. "I didn't expect to see you here today."

"I didn't know that you paid such close attention to every visitor to your farm."

"Oh, but I have a vested interest," Blake said. He slid out of the saddle and brushed off his hands on his jeans. "I hoped I might give you a tour, show you why selling the property to me would benefit the Ryder Hill community."

"Sorry, I'm just here to purchase some fruit. I have a lot to do this afternoon so I'll have to bow out this time," she said, sliding a glance Matthew's way. He bit back a smile.

Connor reached over to snatch the hat off Blake's head and plopped it on his own. Blake's smile withered for a moment. "Careful there, son. That's a genuine Stetson." He and Matthew extracted it from Connor's grip, then Matthew put his son to stand by his side. Blake wasn't comfortable around children and it showed. He chuckled nervously and set his hat firmly on his head. "Enjoy whatever you gather on us," he said. "I'll be seeing you." His tone came off as a warning, which seemed rather odd to Torryn.

After dinner, Connor had just gone up to brush his teeth when Matthew received word that the court intended to move up the auction date of her mother's house and land to the end of June. It was a move he felt Blake had initiated himself. It was more than coincidental that Blake's cousin was the bank manager.

Small-town woes.

Panic bubbled up and overflowed, right along with all her doubts. She pushed aside her almost empty dinner plate, gripped the chair and clutched her stomach. All the jobs she had wouldn't bring in nearly enough funds by that time. The temptation to call her siblings for help washed over her. She knew her mother had meant well, but her faith in Torryn had been misplaced. She drew in several deep breaths.

Her chin wobbled. "It's over. Even if I doubled my

gigs, I wouldn't make enough money in time." Slumping her shoulders, she said, "There's a limit to how much I can do."

Matthew scooted next to her at the kitchen table. "You're forgetting we have a God who is limitless. A God who uses weapons like locusts and boils. A God who speaks and calms the seas."

"I see your point but I don't need locusts or boils. I need cold, hard cash." She jumped out of her chair, scraped the remnants of her meal into the trash and then put it in the sink.

Covering her face with her hands, she murmured, "What am I going to do? How am I going to tell Tess and Nigel that I lost Mom's house? How can I ever look myself in the mirror again knowing that I failed?"

"So many questions. You know that there's really only one answer," Matthew said, wrapping his fingers around hers. He had such strong, firm hands.

It took her a moment to realize that he meant prayer. "Yes, of course…" Her face heated as she joined hands with him and closed her eyes.

Clearing his throat, Matthew began. "Father, we come to You because we believe that You are in control of all things and that You can work them together for our good. You said that if we have a need, we only have to ask. And so we come asking You for faith and for a way to save the Emerson home. In Jesus's name, we pray. Amen."

"Amen."

At the end of the prayer, Matthew gave her a hug. For a second, she welcomed his strength, his calm, his certainty. It was nice having him to lean on and to help to ground her through prayer.

Eyeing the clock, Torryn yawned. "I could use some sleep but I'd better get the cakes in the oven first." Though her legs felt like lead, she trudged over to the kitchen island and set the oven to preheat.

"How can I help?" Matthew asked.

"You don't have to. I'm already invading your space enough as it is already."

"Your being here is not an invasion. It feels good to have this kitchen used as it was when Eloise was alive. Seeing you bustling about brings energy into this home. It used to be so…sterile. Now, there's noise and warmth, and at times I'm avoiding LEGOs all over the place, but I'm loving every moment of it. A huge part of that is you. Connor is happy with you here."

Torryn beamed at his compliment. Matthew certainly had a way with words. But he needed the gift of gab in his profession. She couldn't forget that. Torryn fussed with her curls, then peered up at him. "Did you mean what you just said?" she asked him, and she went to wash the dishes at the sink.

"Of course, I do. If Connor's happy, I'm happy."

"He's a special little boy."

Matthew came up next to her to help her rinse and dry. "I agree. If it weren't for Connor, I don't know how I would have made it through after my wife died. Being a parent gives you resilience, you know?"

She didn't know, of course, but Torryn nodded.

Performing the mundane chore together felt rather intimate, especially when his hand kept bumping against hers. She jerked her hand away, hoping he didn't notice how jittery she was being in such close proximity to him.

"Don't you have to finish getting Connor ready for bed?" she asked.

"Yes, but it won't take long. He's pretty tuckered out." Matthew excused himself to get Connor settled.

Just then, the oven beeped. It was finally at the desired temperature. Torryn busied herself with greasing the baking pans. Then she prepared and poured in the batter before slipping the pans inside the oven. Releasing a plume of air, she turned on the timer. That's when she heard the sounds of something being shuffled across the floor and Matthew appeared with a huge box, dragging it into the kitchen.

"This was delivered late yesterday but I put it into the garage so Connor wouldn't see it until I could set it up."

"What's in it?" She gasped. "Is it his birthday?"

"No, he'll be five next January. I just got this for him because…well, you'll see." He grabbed a box cutter out of the junk drawer and slit the box open down the middle. Tilting the box on its side, Matthew tugged out a full kitchen play set.

"That is so cute," she said, bending over to inspect it. There were tiny sterling silver pots and utensils. "This makes the ones we had as kids look like child's play."

"Yeah, I agree. It is pretty cool." He picked up a toy spatula and examined it before putting it down. "I ordered play food, some baking supplies and an apron. They should come in a few days." He blushed. "I got a little carried away, I guess. But I'm trying to come up with things for us to do together that don't involve just watching television."

"That's such a great idea," Torryn said, as they worked together preparing the icing for the cakes and cleaning the rest of the kitchen. As soon as they finished, she continued their conversation.

"I love that you embrace Connor's interests," she said, clasping her hands to her chest. "It's all about treasuring every moment because life has a way of lifing and we have no choice but to deal with what it brings us. But at least we have our faith to keep us grounded."

"I agree. I've always found release in my praise. It's been a minute since I've sung, though."

She cocked her head. "What's stopping you?"

"I haven't since... Er, I'm rusty."

After wiping her hands on her apron, she placed a hand on her hip. "Well, let's hear it."

He rolled back on his heels. "You expect me to sing now? Here?"

"Yes." She nodded. "No time like the present, I always say."

"I don't know about this..." he hedged, placing his palms flat on the counter right by her baking spoons. The clink of a spoon falling to the floor diverted their attention. She went to help him at the same time he was lowering himself to retrieve it. They bumped heads. "I'm sorry. Are you alright?" he asked, holding her arm.

"Y-yes. I'm fine." She waved a hand. "I shouldn't have put you on the spot. I have a bad habit of speaking my mind. But I was trying to focus on something else rather than the elephant in the room."

He scrunched his nose. "Okay, you're going to have to elaborate because I'm not following you."

"You dropped that bombshell news about the need for a paternity test and since then it's been...crickets."

"That's because I don't like to focus on the past, on

Eloise's indiscretion. It shouldn't dictate the rest of my life."

"That's your prerogative, of course, but this impacts Connor."

"How?" he challenged. "Connor is loved and cared for and he only needs happy memories of his mother."

This was a good time to tell him what Connor had shared about Matthew not talking about Eloise. "I think you should know that—" Suddenly, her cell phone rang. It wasn't a number she recognized, but it might be a potential business call. She couldn't afford to reject those, so she excused herself to respond. It was the church secretary, Janet Hastings, calling to order a few of her cakes. She'd had a slice of cake at Mr. Rodney's and wanted some for the upcoming luncheon for Sunday, the second week in June, to celebrate their pastor's return from Ghana. Since it was last-minute, Janet told her that she planned to compensate her very well. Matthew motioned to her that he was going to put Connor to bed. She gave him a thumbs-up, hoping they could continue their conversation later on.

"Oh, that sounds wonderful. I can throw in some chocolate tarts if you'd like." She searched the drawer for a pad and pencil to write everything down, and then repeated it back to Janet to make sure she had everything correct.

"Yes, that would be fantastic. You can bill the church. See you Sunday." She hung up and Torryn did a happy dance as excitement mingled with hope flowed through her.

By the time Matthew returned, she had decided to broach the topic of Connor and his mother at another time. Instead, she focused her attention on the baking business that seemed to be doing very well. Matthew appeared relieved that she'd changed the subject. "I think you should put an ad in the paper."

"I will." Hope flared in her chest as an idea appeared. "The church luncheon," she said.

"What about it?"

"It's the perfect place to hand out flyers advertising my goods. I'll check with the event coordinator to see if that's okay."

Matthew's eyes brightened. "Brilliant... They might be even more motivated if you phrased it as a sort of fundraiser to save your mother's property. Then if you charge a good rate for your cakes and goods, you'll make the money you need even more quickly."

"That's actually a great idea." She bit her bottom lip. "But what if Tess questions why I'm trying to raise money when there is an inheritance?"

"Keep it generic, like a fundraiser for a good cause in Ruth's honor. Once it's over, you can share the truth with Tess and Nigel if you want."

Her mouth widened into a grin. She pointed upward. "You were right. Prayer works and I feel inspired." She placed a hand on her hip. "You know what? I'll call Janet back and ask right now. Why wait?" Five minutes later, she ended the call and high-fived Matthew. "Janet is going to announce the fundraiser at the luncheon. I can't wait for Sunday. Maybe the church will let me use their kitchen, if it's big enough." She tapped her chin. "I'll need an assistant, though."

"I'll help and maybe you can recruit someone at the event? Most of the town will be there."

"Yes, that makes sense and thank you for volunteering. I might take you up on that. A retiree or college student would be ideal." She clasped her hands. "I might actually be able to do this. I might be able to save my mother's house," she exclaimed, jumping up and down before making herself go still. She released a long breath of air. "I can't get ahead of myself. I have to wait to see if I get orders but this could actually happen."

"You will," Matthew said, coming around to hug her. "You're going to do it, Torryn. You're going to save your mother's house and keep it out of Blake's clutches, and I'll be right there to rejoice with you."

"Can we pray on this again?" she asked shyly, holding out her hands.

"Of course, I'd be more than happy to."

After they said, "Amen," she nestled into him and allowed herself to hope, to believe, that she wouldn't fail. For the first time in her life, she truly believed she could finish what she had started and be a success. She would make her mother proud and she would be proud of herself to boot.

Resting her head against his chest, hearing his steady heartbeat, Torryn closed her eyes and smiled. It was all coming together and she had Matthew to thank for it.

Chapter Eleven

When the town pastor, who just happened to be his brother-in-law and best friend, reached out to Matthew and said that he wanted to see him, there was no way to avoid it. Pastor Garth Harland, who had been away in Ghana on a mission trip for the past few months, had texted Matthew to let him know he had returned and that they should get together and catch up. Matthew had promised to stop by the church on his way home the next day.

Pulling into the parking lot, he took in all the perennials lining the walkway. There were two rosebushes in bloom on either side of the path leading up to the entrance of the church. The landscaping was incredible, and the scents were glorious. Besides Garth's car, there was only one other vehicle parked in the church parking lot.

After getting out of his SUV, Matthew headed toward the church's garden. In the midst of all the different flowers in bloom was a bench dedicated to the previous minister. Before Eloise had become too ill to venture out to church, they had often spent hours after the service sitting out here talking to God and to each other.

Garth was sitting on that bench.

"Welcome back, brother," Matthew said, greeting his friend since ninth grade. The two had sat next to each other in algebra class and had been inseparable until Garth's younger sister, Eloise, had asked him out when they were in college.

Garth stood to hug him. "It's good to be home." They sat on the bench angled so they faced each other. "How's my nephew?"

"At least three inches taller since you saw him last." Matthew pulled up recent pictures of Connor on his phone to show him.

"Wow. He is solid. Seems like we've got another future linebacker in the family." He flexed his muscles. "Glad to know he'll continue my legacy." Garth was six-four with a brute strength that had made him a great offensive player to Matthew's quarterback. But instead of heading to the NFL, Garth had focused on becoming a pediatrician before he was called into ministry.

However, he still used his medical skills during his mission trips. Garth was a solid human being and friend. And as much of an overachiever as Matthew and as his sister, until she'd passed.

Matthew studied his son's picture intently before giving Garth a playful shove. "You're right. I didn't even notice how much Connor takes after you. I hope he doesn't get your ugly mug." There was secret relief that Garth had established a stronger physical resemblance to Eloise's side of the family. Connor had the same hazel eyes as Eloise and Garth. Mentioning that familial trait was intentional on Garth's part. Eloise had told her brother about her indiscretion when she learned she was pregnant. Garth had urged her to confess.

That truth bomb had created an understandable awkwardness between the men. How could you vent to your friend when his sister was the one who had hurt you? Garth had navigated that slippery slope with God's help, which led to him being instrumental in saving Matthew and Eloise's marriage.

"How have you been?" Garth prodded. "I know you haven't been attending services in my absence."

"I haven't lost my faith, if that's what you're asking," Matthew said. "I just don't know who this mystery person is and the thought that he could be in the congregation laughing in my face all the while knowing he slept with my wife is untenable. The thought that it could be someone I know, someone I trust… A Judas in the midst. Before him, Eloise and I were each other's first, one and only. This man ruined that." He shook his head. "It weighs on me."

"I know it's difficult, man. But you forgave Eloise. You have to forgive this person as well, even if you never find out who he is."

"I know. That's the one thing I haven't surrendered. It's because it's making me question my place in Connor's life. He could take him away from me." Resentment filled Matthew's chest. "At any moment, he could demand to be in Connor's life, and I wouldn't be able to stop him."

"You still need to forgive."

Matthew simply nodded. "I'll have to pray on that."

"There's a way to get that boulder off your chest," Garth said. "You need to read the paternity-test results. There's no doubt in my mind that you're Connor's father."

Matthew bunched his fists. "I feel that in my heart

but if it isn't the case…there would be no going back. I couldn't unknow the truth. So I prefer to dwell in the in-between space, between knowing and not knowing."

"Suit yourself, but if it were me, I'd want to know. When God says the truth sets you free it's because it would set you free from sleepless nights."

His mouth popped open. "How did you know?"

"I know you," Garth said with a lopsided grin.

"There's something you don't know. I lost the results."

The pastor's eyes widened. "How did you manage to do that?"

"I misplaced it somewhere and I've searched high and low but I can't find it. I even asked Torryn—his babysitter—and she said she hasn't seen it." He filled in Garth on all that had transpired, that he was still searching for the letter, but figured it had somehow ended up in the trash. Garth suggested he take another test, but Matthew disagreed. "Maybe this is a sign that I don't need to know."

"Whatever you decide, I'll be here and I'll keep you in my prayers." He paused for a moment, then asked, "Who's Torryn?"

"She's one of Ruth Emerson's daughters. And she's watching Connor when I'm at work. She's really wonderful with him. And he loves her."

"Is it just him?"

The question hit him square in the chest. "We've become friends, but I'm not looking to start dating her…or anyone," he sputtered. "A man can have a female friend."

"I'm just teasing you, man." Garth laughed. "I did hear talk about you spending time with a lady friend. That was the first thing I heard about once I was back."

He pinned Matthew with a pointed stare. "If that rumor is true, that would be great. Because you have every right to find love again. To move on. And Connor could use a mother."

Unwilling to finish the rest of this conversation, Matthew stood. "I'd better get going." He missed Torryn but no way would he admit that to his friend.

"Wait. Before you go, I have something I need to ask you." Garth placed a hand on Matthew's arm to keep him from leaving. "I wanted to ask you to sing 'Great is Thy Faithfulness' for me at the church luncheon on Sunday. It would mean a lot to me if you did."

Matthew shifted. "I don't know. I haven't sung that song since…" He stared at a cardinal landing on the flower bush near the bench.

"Did you hear that I got really sick while I was in Ghana? The doctors said it was life-threatening, but I was in a coma and didn't know it."

"What? No. I hadn't heard about that." Chills ran down his spine at the thought that he could have lost his best friend in addition to his wife.

"Yes, but when I was in the hospital I remember being in pain and then the words of that song came to me. It saw me through my lowest moment and that's why I'd like you to sing it." He drew in a deep breath before he continued, his tone grave. "But I understand if you don't feel up to it. I'll just—"

Matthew pursed his lips. "Emotional blackmail? Really?"

Garth arched an eyebrow. "But is it working?"

"Yes. You forget that I know you."

"It's just that if you don't sing, then Sister Janet is going to sing one of her originals."

"Now, we get to the bottom of things." The men shared a laugh, then Matthew grew serious. "I am so thankful that God saw you through your illness—" his voice broke "—because I couldn't bear the thought of losing you." Matthew squared his shoulders. "I'd be honored to sing at the luncheon. Just don't laugh if I'm off-key or I can't hit the note."

"Oh, no doubt about it. I am going to laugh so you'd better practice."

Matthew snickered. "What would your congregation say if they heard you talking like this? You don't sound very pastoral right now."

Garth got up and put him in a headlock briefly. "They would say it sounds just like something I'd say."

"Yes, they sure would. You know the older church sisters want to give you the boot for your 'unprincipled ways.'"

"That's because they knew me back when I was stomping around in diapers." Garth mopped his brow. "But I'm going to be the best me God wants me to be. And that's what I want for you."

After a quick prayer, the men parted ways. Matthew thought a lot about what Garth had said about letting go of the past. If he was ever going to have a healthy relationship, he needed to make room in his heart. And that meant forgiving Eloise and moving on with his life.

Was he ready for that?

Matthew pondered that all the way home. When he steered into the driveway, Torryn and Connor were coming around from the side of the house, garden hose in hand. Every morning and afternoon, they made sure to water the plants, including the sunflowers they'd planted.

Torryn waved at him and gave him a bright smile as if she was happy to see him, as if she was waiting for him to come home.

Home.

The picture Connor drew of the four sunflowers flashed in his mind.

Connor was jumping up and down and yelling *Daddy* as if he hadn't seen him in days instead of the few hours since lunch. He got out of his SUV and studied the two people standing before him.

Both of them were completely soaked, including Torryn's apron. Her hair was sticking up in all directions and Connor's curls drooped down the sides of his face. They had never looked cuter.

Both of them.

Torryn said, "The sunflower seeds finally sprouted today. Do you want to check them out?"

His heart skipped a beat. What was going on here? It wasn't just the sunflower seeds sprouting. Something was spreading deep within him. Immediately, he blamed Garth for putting ideas in his head.

Who was he kidding? Garth had only voiced what he himself knew to be true. He just hadn't wanted to acknowledge that something was building between him and Torryn. Well, at least on his part. He wasn't sure about her.

She narrowed her eyes. "Hello-o-o?"

Although, judging by the red hue on her cheeks... it might be mutual. He stepped forward. She seemed surprised.

"Daddy, come see the sunflowers." Connor pulled on his leg and snapped him out of his reverie. Dragging his eyes away from Torryn, Matthew made his way over to the flower bed.

"Look, Daddy. The flowers are growing." Connor ran from side to side. "It's going to get taller than me."

Matthew took a picture with his phone. "It's hard to imagine that this tiny sprout is going to become something so beautiful in a matter of weeks." He looked over at Torryn to see her glancing at him. Yes, she knew he wasn't just talking about the plants.

She sidled next to him as they stared at the sprouts. After a moment, she said softly, "It is a wonder, isn't it? The realization that something you thought was dead is very much alive."

Their shoulders touched.

Matthew drew in a deep breath.

His pulse raced. And his heart somersaulted. Then he slowly took her hand in his.

It was then—only then—that he exhaled.

Torryn packed up the back of Matthew's trunk with cakes, tarts and muffins for the church luncheon. She didn't know how she was still awake, when she'd been up in the wee hours of the morning decorating the three-tiered apple-cinnamon cake. She remembered praying... *Lord, help me get one more layer done. Lord, help me get the filling just right.*

Torryn had gone above and beyond by adding fresh fruit as the filling and as a garnish. The exhaustion had her questioning her ambitions, but the end result was a show-stopper. She had ended her dog-walking business and paused her consignment agreement with Mr. Rodney to focus on this luncheon. Matthew agreed with her decision. She saw it as the proverbial putting all her eggs in one basket, or in this case, all her cakes on one table.

Matthew walked over holding the last of the tarts. He was dressed in a pair of dark slacks and a light blue dress shirt. She would change out of her pants and T-shirt and into a sundress after she'd finished the delivery.

Janet had swung by earlier in the day to get Connor so he could play with the other children at the bounce house and waterslide the church had set up. Matthew had Connor's change of clothes hanging in the passenger seat along with her dress.

With the deadline looming, Torryn had been grateful for the respite from watching Connor, and she had accomplished a lot, though she did miss Connor's questions. Without his presence, the house was quiet. Too quiet. It left her time to reflect on that moment between her and Matthew by the sunflower sprouts more times than she would care to count.

It had been fleeting. So why was she dwelling on it? Matthew hadn't given any signs that it meant more to him than a shared connection between friends. But he'd held her hand. That had to mean something, right?

Matthew placed the tarts next to the other containers and stood back. "I have no idea how you are still standing after doing all this baking. What time did you go to bed?"

She chuckled. "I haven't yet. I'm riding off coffee, Mountain Dew and nonstop prayers."

He wiped his brow. "I believe you. I'm sorry I couldn't hang." Once the college student she had hired left, Matthew had jumped in to help chop fruit, while Connor played in the kitchen next to them. Most of the baking had been done the night before because she didn't have storage and the church hadn't been able to accommodate her since they were using their kitchen space to prep the food for the luncheon.

As much as they wanted the fundraiser to be a success, enough space to prepare everything would be an issue. But she would cross that bridge when they got there.

"Nonsense. You were a great help to me, and you continue to open your home to me for free. Plus, you helped me order the flyers and those fancy order cards. I feel like I have a legit baking business now."

"That's the idea," he said, giving her a smile before closing the trunk.

She lowered her gaze. "I have to leave, eventually. I can't stay in Ryder Hill."

"I do hope you change your mind."

It was unlikely. Unless he gave her a reason to stay. She couldn't continue to live next door to him and fuel her crush. Yes, she had finally admitted to herself that she was growing to care for Matthew.

When he'd held her hand, it had warmed her insides, giving her all the feels.

Then he said, "It still doesn't stop me from hoping you'll change your mind," and his gray eyes drew her in. He gave her arm a squeeze. "I see that you're nervous about today, but people are going to love your baked goods. You'll see. You're going to thrive, and you'll make the money you need."

How did he know how affected she was in his presence? If only he hadn't grabbed her hand with his, she wouldn't be wishing for more.

However, she wasn't about to correct him, and the only way to keep from blurting out the truth about her feelings was to keep moving. "We'd better get going," she said, glancing at her watch. "I need time to set up my display." *And to normalize my breathing.*

Matthew made his way to the driver's side and she to the passenger side, when he paused. "Do you want to drive?"

"What? No!"

He tossed the keys her way. "It would be a boss move, driving up to the luncheon."

"I'm already a boss. I don't need validation." She tossed them back. They had been practicing daily but Torryn lacked the confidence—Matthew used the word *motivation*—to venture onto the main road.

"Okay, I won't push you." He jumped into the SUV and started up the engine. Before he pulled off, Matthew held her hand in his and prayed. "Lord, we have a plan in place, the first step. We ask for Your increase. In Jesus's name. Amen."

They arrived at the church, pulling up at the rear of the building so they could unload by the kitchen entrance. Eyeing the bounce house and waterslide located by the corner of the field behind the church, Torryn said, "If I had the time, I would get in."

Matthew chuckled. "I would join you."

Torryn believed him. She looked at Matthew and smiled. How did she ever think him stuffy? There was a fun-loving man under all those stiff suits, and she was loving getting to know him.

"Maybe later," she whispered.

Janet came over, wearing a chiffon blue dress and black pumps. "There you are. Right on time. Connor is with the other children getting cleaned up in the Sunday school classroom." Matthew handed her Connor's change of clothes. Her eyebrows shot up when she saw all the baked goods in the trunk. "My word, Torryn Emerson, you have indeed outdone yourself. These look marvelous. Far beyond anything I envisioned."

Torryn's face warmed. "That's what you can expect from me."

Janet sniffed the air. "They smell simply delightful."

Matthew chimed in, "I can attest that they taste as good as they look and smell."

"I'll be sure to find out." Janet splayed her hands. "I'll leave you to it."

Matthew directed Torryn to go inside and begin dressing the cake and desserts tables while he brought everything inside. For once, Torryn didn't argue. Together they placed everything just so. Twenty minutes later, it was all ready.

Matthew placed the flyers and order cards on the end of the table. "Get ready," he told her. "You're going to be a huge success."

Chapter Twelve

"There's no place like home," Pastor Garth said as he stood before the congregation, who had all gathered inside the sanctuary after the luncheon, which had been a success. All that was left of the baked goods that Torryn had made were crumbs.

In preparation for his song, Matthew had stolen away when everyone was outside to practice the melody one more time. When he had finished, he stayed by the piano in the sanctuary as people trickled inside.

The crowd broke into applause at the pastor's words.

"For many this is a cliché, but for me, this is my truth." The pastor's voice broke. Heartful murmurs rippled through the crowd. Garth began to share what he had told Matthew about his illness and recovery in Ghana. Garth was a gifted preacher so the room quieted to listen to his tale. Everyone had come out to hear the pastor's testimony, including the fire chief, Justin Washington, and Blake Whitlock. Matthew had been shocked to see them as they weren't regular church attendees, but then again, he hadn't been either the past few months.

"If it weren't for God's grace and mercies, I wouldn't be standing here. One thing I can tell you is that when you're facing death, you're thinking the most about the people who matter in your life. You're thinking about the people you love, and you worry, did you love them enough? Did you do all that you can?" The pastor scanned the audience. "If your answer to any of those two questions are no, then you have work to do. God's answer is always yes. Yes, He loved us enough to give His only son. Yes, He loved us to throw all our flaws in the sea of forgetfulness and cleanse us of all unrighteousness."

"Amen," Matthew said, along with the other congregants.

His fingers rested on the piano keys, as he waited for Garth to finish his speech to the crowd. Torryn had chosen to sit next to Tess a few rows from the back, and for once Connor was not snuggled up to her. He was with the other children in the first rows on the side of the sanctuary, situated between two boys, Abe and Sam. All three of them were swinging their legs. Connor had told him they were his best friends.

A pang hit his heart. He should not have stayed away from church for so long. For Connor's sake and his own.

"The thing is, God was with me and He is with you. Throughout all our trials, our ups and downs and run-arounds, He is there. The enemy would have us believe that we are alone, so could isolate ourselves but that is the furthest thing from the truth. God whispers through His word, through our brothers and sisters, and through song." He turned in Matthew's direction. Matthew began to play the interlude low while Garth continued talking. "I would have been consumed had it not been for God's love. He is ever faithful and He specializes in second chances. There was a song that got me through my toughest time. And I'm blessed to have a best friend who knows how to carry a tune, because trust me, you don't want me to bellow it out."

The congregation snickered. Pointing at Matthew, Garth said, "Welcome Brother Matthew as he honors God through the song 'Great is Thy Faithfulness.'"

Matthew adjusted the volume on the piano before turning on the microphone. He leaned forward and started to sing. "Great is Thy faithfulness, oh, God my Father." Matthew's voice echoed through the church, which jarred him. He stopped singing and cleared his throat. "Forgive me, it's been a while that I've sung."

"You've got this," someone shouted.

He closed his eyes and sang, pouring his heart out before God. The crowd rejoiced with him as he sang the refrain and the other verses. The musicians began on the keyboard, the drums and the saxophone, and the choir took over and began to sing while Matthew played and played.

His heart lifted.

Matthew put down the mic, shot to his feet and splayed his hands wide. A strong pair of arms encircled his shoulders and Matthew welcomed Garth's prayers on his behalf.

When Garth moved on to pray for others who came up to the altar, Matthew sought out Connor. His blessing. Connor was jumping and dancing with the other boys, his eyes full of happiness, which expanded Matthew's sense of peace. Next, he searched out the crowd until he found Torryn. She had her eyes closed and her hands lifted high in worship as she belted out the words along with everyone else.

And that's when the truth hit him.

She meant more than a friend to him. Much more. And he was going to finally let go and let God work that out in His time. In His way.

"I had no idea you could sing like that," Torryn told Matthew when they drove home that evening. She couldn't get over his beautiful voice. Connor was asleep in the back, his head lolling to the side.

"Yeah, well, I had fancied myself becoming the next gospel singer, like Donnie McClurkin or Fred Hammond but my mother insisted I get my law degree to preserve my father's legacy. That's her favorite way to keep me in line."

"I take it that is a bone of contention between the two of you?"

"It has been. It certainly was when it came to my singing. My dear mother liked to inform me that while I was a very good singer, I wasn't *that* good. So I needed to focus on my law studies instead."

"Whoa. That wasn't very kind of her."

"If you were to get to know my mother, you would see that Peggy Lawson does not bite her tongue. She's quite adept at making her opinions known. Kind of like someone else I know." He winked at her. "In this case, though, she was right. I persuaded Garth to accompany me to New York for an audition. There were at least fifty other guys my age there and they were all extremely talented."

"Really? That sounds like a lot of competition." She toyed with her curls, while caught up in Matthew's story.

"Yep. And, the thing is, while you're waiting your turn, you have to sit through the other auditions. You get to hear the enormous talent you're competing with. It's quite daunting."

"Yes, but you have to believe in yourself," Torryn said. "You can't let the voices of those around you drown out your purpose."

His lips quirked. "I wish I had known you back then. You would have done wonders for my confidence. Instead, I was saddled with Garth, who would gasp or get bug-eyed after each performance and say, 'Yo, you've got to step up your game, bro. 'Cause you don't stand a chance.'"

She cracked up and covered her mouth. "What kind of a support system was that?"

"Yep. He was the worst, and unapologetic about it. As you can imagine, I was doomed."

"So what happened when it was your turn to sing?" Her heart was already aching for the sad outcome. Torryn pictured a young Matthew leaving the audition thoroughly devastated.

Matthew focused on the road. "Er, I won."

Her mouth dropped. "Say what?"

"Yes, I killed it. When my name was called, I went up there, kept it simple and stuck to the song. I didn't try to outsing or outriff any of the other dudes there. I decided to be just me and I gave my best."

For some reason that made her heart swoon. "Oh, I am loving this story, Matthew. And if this is an indication of you in court, I must hear you try a case one day."

"That's high praise, Torryn, but I'm afraid you would be sorely disappointed. My estate cases are mundane. Dry, even."

"I don't think you could bore me. Ever. Anything you have to say, I want to hear it."

He blushed at her words.

Was she spreading it on too thick with that compliment? She wished she could scoop those words right back into her mouth and swallow them. Torryn had never been one to temper her words or hide her emotions. But this friendship with Matthew required more finesse than she was used to. She didn't want him thinking that she was infatuated. Even if it was true.

"So if you won, why wasn't your face on a billboard somewhere? I would have remembered if you were a teen heartthrob."

His talent was off-the-charts. He had the kind of voice she wouldn't get tired of hearing. If she was his wife, she would be nagging him to sing all the time. Whoa. She zipped that thought pattern closed. She wasn't Matthew's wife and she wasn't looking to be, no matter how good it felt to do things with him and Connor, talk with him, laugh with him.

"I found out they didn't want just my face on the billboard." It took a moment for his words to sink in. She tried to contain her laughter. "Then when I read the contract and saw that I would owe the label all that they'd invested in me if I didn't get a number-one hit, I hightailed it home and went back to law school."

"Smart move." She tapped his arm, hating that she noticed how strong his muscle felt under her hand.

"I can one-hundred-percent say that I have no regrets. So did you notice that all your order cards got filled? The fundraiser is a big hit."

Even now, she couldn't believe how supportive the

townspeople had been. Most families had ordered two to three different kinds of cakes and some had already paid her through a money-transfer app or with checks. That was more than she had hoped for.

"Yes." She beamed. "I have to call tomorrow and see if Pattie's Pastries is available for rent and I'll have to get two assistants to help me fulfill the orders. I'm putting everything I've made so far into this investment, so I hope it will pay off."

He frowned. "That's quite a risk you're taking. You need to be making money, not spending it."

"Yes, but I need a bigger space and sometimes you have to invest money to make money." Though his concern caused her to worry. The sudden possibility that this attempt might fail, the way her other business had, made her stomach churn with doubt.

"Hang on, that place is up for rent? I thought that it was for sale."

"Tess said someone purchased the building and there's a For Rent sign on the door. I could use a professional kitchen to meet the demands of such large orders," she breathed out, holding the building panic at bay.

"Oh, I hadn't noticed the sign." He pulled into her driveway. It gave her pause that he wasn't going to his house. She had gotten used to spending most of her time over there. A loud snore came from the back seat. Both Torryn and Matthew cracked up. "Connor's getting in some good sleep. I don't think he'll have any nightmares tonight."

"That would be a relief, I'm sure. Has he still been having them a lot?" she asked.

Matthew cocked his head for a moment. "No. In fact,

I don't think he's had one since…that day you planted the sunflowers in the yard."

She got out of his SUV and he did as well, leaving the engine running so Connor could benefit from the AC. It was muggy out.

Stepping closer to Matthew, she decided it was time to talk about Connor. "I've been meaning to tell you… The day we planted the sunflowers, Connor talked to me about his mother. He even showed me her photograph. Connor thinks you're mad at him if he talks about her."

He shook his head and rubbed his chin. "I don't understand why he would think that."

"Because you don't talk about her."

"I don't because it's too painful for Connor. I don't like seeing him cry or get upset. But I don't exclude her on purpose. I'm the one who put his mother's picture by his bed."

"Have you ever thought that he *needs* to cry? He *needs* to let out those emotions?"

"Of course, I have," he said, through gritted teeth. "Who do you think rocks him for hours when he cries out for his mother? I did put him in therapy to help him through the grief process."

"And all that is commendable, but maybe—just maybe—you decided for him when his grief should end."

"I did no such thing. I might not have encouraged conversation but I didn't discourage it, either."

"True. But he's four years old and his mother is gone and never coming back." Her breath hitched. "You don't know what it's like to be so young, looking out the window, waiting up in bed, thinking you're in a dream and your mother will return someday."

Matthew's face softened, suddenly filled with compassion. "No, I don't know what it's like." He sighed. "You're right, Torryn. I did dictate when Connor's grief should end, even though I didn't realize that was what I was doing. I was grieving, too, but I spent time with Eloise in the hospital. I held her hand when she drew her last breath. Connor didn't see any of that. I shielded him. All Connor saw was his mother healthy and happy, and then she was gone." He rubbed his temples. "That is a lot to process." His shoulders slumped. "Poor little guy."

Reaching over, he wiped her cheek with his thumb, even though she hadn't noticed she was crying. "And you had to face that twice. I'm so sorry, Torryn. How did you get through?"

"My faith. My family." She tilted her head back to look into his eyes. "My friends."

"This friendship means a lot to me and I know Connor adores you. But as Connor's father, I know I need to spend more quality time with him. You have a lot going on now but when things settle down a bit, could you teach me how to make cupcakes? I was thinking that it's something Connor and I could do together."

"I'd be happy to teach you," she said.

He rested a hand on her arm. "Thank you for being honest with me, Torryn. For making me see things in such a different light. I'm glad Connor has you, but it seems as though he could benefit from more therapy. I'll call the counselor tomorrow to make Connor an appointment. I want him to be the healthiest little boy he can be despite his tremendous loss."

Matthew placed a gentle kiss on her forehead, then

waved goodbye to her, got in the SUV and drove off. Torryn lost track of how long she stood there, in front of the guesthouse, thinking of all they'd said to each other.

Chapter Thirteen

We shouldn't pick and choose whom we forgive, Matthew mused. God extended forgiveness to all and He expected us to do the same. Matthew knew God's position on the matter, and over the past few mornings had centered his Bible devotion on forgiveness, hoping it would remove the wedge from his heart.

Maybe it would be easier if he knew whom he was supposed to forgive. The fact that he still hadn't found the paternity-results letter fueled his anger even more. Though he believed that it had been thrown away, he had still searched Connor's bedroom and the living room just in case, but it had been to no avail.

As Matthew stood in the bathroom brushing his teeth, he sighed. He was getting tired of being angry. At his late wife. At the man she cheated on him with. At God. At life in general. Anger was exhausting him and he was ready to move forward.

He went into his bedroom and dropped to his knees. "Lord, I give all these feelings of anger and pain and inadequacy over to You. I thank You for forgiving me and I'm going to follow Your example. I forgive this man, whoever he is, and I leave his judgment in Your hands." He sobbed as he let go and surrendered all his pain over to God.

When he got back to his feet, Matthew vowed to dwell on it no more. Once he had gotten dressed for work, he went into Connor's bedroom to wake him.

Connor had spent another night in his own bed and there had been no nightmares. His latest therapy session with Dr. Keisha Vernon had gone well. *Thank You, God.* His son looked so peaceful that he hated to wake him, but Matthew had a client meeting early that morning. Matthew had set his appointments that way because Connor had a play date with Abe and Sam later that day at Sky Zone, an indoor trampoline park.

Matthew would host the boys the next time.

And while Connor was on his play date, Matthew hoped to be on one of his own. With Torryn. He was hoping to drum up the courage to ask her out on a date. He hadn't been on a first date in close to seven years, so he planned to keep it simple, low-key but fun. He had given it a lot of thought and had settled on fishing since it was something they both liked. Or maybe he would be adventurous and suggest roller skating. He would let Torryn decide. If she actually wanted to go out with him.

The whole time it took for Connor to get dressed and for Matthew to get him out the door and to the bakery, Connor spoke about his play date. And his son's excitement was infectious. No doubt, Matthew would be just as thrilled if he also had a date to anticipate.

When they entered the bakery, Matthew was surprised at the whirl of activity. Torryn was standing by a huge mixer and one of the assistants was pouring in flour. Another assistant was at a table squeezing icing on finished cakes. Boxes lined the rear table with labels that said *Torryn's Treats.*

Her hair, shirt and shoes had flecks of flour, and she looked adorable and happy. Connor yelled out for her. It was then that Matthew realized he hadn't packed Connor a lunch or toys... He didn't know how Torryn was going to manage with him underfoot, especially since she had so many orders to fulfill.

She spun around. "Hey, Connor," she said, taking off her plastic gloves and coming over to give his son a high five. She peered at Matthew from under her lashes before averting her gaze. Ever since he'd kissed her forehead, Torryn had been acting shy around him.

"Are you sure that you're okay with keeping him here?" Matthew asked. "I can take him to work with me."

"Yes, I've got a space cleared for him." She scurried off, with Connor gripping her hand. In the far corner on an area rug, there was a toy kitchen, a little television, a small cot and a child's desk with paper and crayons. Connor screeched before running over to play in the kitchen.

"Wow. You've thought of everything." His heart was full to overflowing right now. The fact that she had considered Connor in this way meant everything to him. It was something a mother would do.

"Of course. I'd do anything for the little guy." She played with her apron strings.

"How are the orders going?" he asked.

She led him over to her desk and pulled out an order log to show him her entries. "The response has been beyond amazing. The deadline for orders was yesterday and according to my calculations, I am going to make eight thousand dollars. That's after supply costs and paying the interns. The interns are learning with me to get credit hours so I'm not required to pay them, but I'll give them both a bonus. Then I'll use the rest to pay off the remainder of my hospital bill."

His mouth dropped. "What? How?"

"Ryder Hill has some of the best townsfolk. A lot paid more than my asking price. I am going to be baking quite a few cakes and special orders over the next few days. But we'll beat the deadline." All he could do was shake his head in amazement. She lifted her hands. "This is nothing but God. He did it." She burst into a jig.

Matthew took her hand and gave her a twirl. "Yes, He did. I'm so happy for you." He drew her in for a hug, then said, "We should celebrate."

She leaned back to look at his face. "What do you have in mind?"

"I was thinking fishing or roller skating." He swallowed, resisting the urge to fidget.

She frowned. "Does Connor know how to skate?"

"I was hoping it would be just the two of us. He actually has a play date this evening, so…"

"Oh." When realization sunk in, her eyes went wide. "Oh!" She exhaled. "You mean like a date?"

He nodded, then began rambling. "I know you're swamped so I understand if this isn't convenient. But I figured I would help you with the orders later today especially since you're making cupcakes and you said you'd teach me. It would be a win-win."

Torryn smiled at him. "I'd love to go out with you."

"You would?" He hugged her again before releasing her. "Well, alright. I'll come by to get you later and we can drop Connor off and then be on our way." Matthew bent down to kiss Connor, then headed toward the door. The quicker he got to work, the quicker he could be back for their date. His hand was on the front-door handle when he stopped. Spinning around, Matthew gasped. He hadn't realized she had been right behind him. "I forgot to ask where you wanted to go."

"It doesn't matter," she said, eyes shining. "As long as I'm with you."

"You got it."

Matthew walked out the door with a spring in his step. There was nothing better than a bold woman. Until Torryn, he hadn't known the value of someone who spoke what was on her mind. Maybe he would do the same and express what was growing in his heart and maybe, just maybe, she felt the same.

"How on earth did you know my shoe size?" Torryn asked as she glided around the curve in the roller rink. Matthew had booked a private sixty-minute session so it was just them with the attendants. Soft music played in the background and they had the lights dimmed with a sparkle of stars sprinkled on the hardwood floor. It was romantic and playful. Perfect for a first date.

After working on orders at the bakery, they had stopped at their respective homes to clean up and change into jeans and T-shirts before heading to the roller rink. Matthew had insisted that she drive. It had been nerve-wracking but since the rink was away from the main road with minimal traffic, she had done it.

"I looked at one of the sandals you left at my house when you ran across the lawn in your bare feet."

She giggled. "How creative. What would you have done if I had said no?"

"But you didn't, so I don't have to think about that."

"Good comeback." She grinned. Then she glided off, going as fast as she could. Matthew kept up with her as best as he could.

"What made you choose roller skating over fishing?" Matthew asked.

"After hours in the kitchen this seemed like a great way to work off some excess energy. It's been years since I've donned a pair of skates. I've been looking forward to this all day." She didn't add that she had also been looking forward to spending time with him. Just the two of them. And she hoped it would be the first of many. As long as they kept things lighthearted, they could spend time together. There was nothing wrong with them enjoying each other's company until her departure at the end of the summer.

Matthew swerved around her and sped ahead. "Try to keep up."

"Challenge accepted." She raced past him and stuck out her tongue. "Especially since I was going easy on you. I'll have you know I was once on the roller skating team for Ryder Hill."

"No need to slow down on my account," he retorted, executing a fancy move. "I didn't even know they had a team."

"Yes, I quit in the tenth grade. But I'm impressed with how good you are. You don't seem the type."

"I wasn't always this stuffy." He laughed. "I do know how to have fun."

"I figured you did. I just didn't think you were the

type to make time for fun." She spun to face him, skating backward. "How about we make this interesting?"

He sidled close to her. He smelled really good, a combination of something spicy and woodsy. It was distracting in a good way. "What do you have in mind?"

"Let's have a race. Three times around the rink."

"Winner gets what?"

"Winner gets the last cupcake from my bag. Decorated by Connor."

"What a priceless reward."

At the count of three, they took off, pushing and shoving each other along the way, followed by plenty of laughter. Each performed mischievous antics as they took the curve to keep the other from progressing. But as they neared the end of the third lap, Matthew pushed slightly ahead.

If he won, he would brag on her for days. Well, she couldn't have that. Reaching over, she grabbed the tail of his shirt and gave it a tug. Matthew toppled backward, taking her down with him. The force of their fall made them slide across the floor together. Together.

"You sabotaged me," Matthew said.

Torryn fell backward and snorted. "All's fair when it comes to the last cupcake." She looked at the ceiling, enjoying the lights and the music. He scooted next to her and folded his arms behind his head. She looked at her watch. "How much time do we have before Connor needs to be picked up?"

"We have about a half hour."

"Do you want to get pizza or something?"

"I could eat."

"Pizza it is."

Matthew stood up and dusted off his jeans before reaching for her hand. After she placed her hand in his, he pulled her to her feet. They glided over to the entrance, returned their skates to the rental area, then went to a nearby pizza place to eat.

"Do we need to get Connor a slice?" she asked, biting into her slice, loving the gooey cheese. Cheese and sauce dripped on her chin and shirt.

He wiped his mouth. "No, he and his buddies are going to eat at the Sky Zone."

"I had a great time hanging with you tonight," she told him. Then she yawned. "I promise you, my yawning isn't a reflection of what I think of you or our date. But I had a long day today, and the same tomorrow, so I'd better get some rest. But I would love for us to do this again."

Matthew stared into her eyes. "Me, too."

After they finished eating, they went to retrieve Connor from his play date at Sky Zone. Connor fell asleep during the ride home. Matthew pulled into her driveway and opened her door for her. She grabbed her purse and dug inside before pulling out the cupcake. "Thank you for a great time. Here you go." After taking it out of the plastic baggie, she handed it to him.

Matthew opened the bag, took two bites and gave her the rest. He had a glob of frosting on his bottom lip. Standing on her tiptoes, she pressed her lips to his. Matthew's arms circled her waist as he deepened the kiss. She rested a hand on his chest and followed his lead.

When they finally pulled away from each other, he said good night, and went back to his car. Torryn walked into her home, her feet light and her heart happy.

Slipping onto the couch, she tucked her feet under

her and reflected on the past few hours. Her date tonight had been wonderful from beginning to end. And it was all because of Matthew. He was a gentleman. He was thoughtful. He was fun. And being with him was…easy. Natural. It was like they were in sync.

Torryn's stomach fluttered. She had already fallen in love with Connor. Was she now falling for his dad?

Chapter Fourteen

P aid in full.

Matthew studied those three words, smiled and leaned back into his chair. Then he snapped a picture and sent it over to Torryn. He had just submitted the check paying the back taxes on Ruth Emerson's home and the bank had updated the balance.

Her response was quick. Squee! Three words I didn't know would ever be on my to-do list, but I am so glad to see the zero balance.

Congratulations. You did it.

She sent a dancing GIF. Matthew hit the like button on it, then sent another message: We should celebrate.

That can be arranged.

See you in twenty minutes?

Matthew packed up his briefcase and said to his assistant, "I probably won't be back today. I'm getting an early start to the weekend and so should you," he said, thinking of the beautiful day. Maybe Torryn will want to go on a hike or something. No, he was going to grill in the backyard, put on some music and finally get on that trampoline with Connor. He rushed to the grocery store and picked up burgers, franks, corn on the cob, rolls and some condiments.

It was close to 90 degrees, so he would set up the mini water slide he had purchased recently. He texted Torryn to let her know of his plans and that he would arrive a few minutes later than originally planned.

When he arrived at the bakery, he saw the For Rent sign was once again on display. As soon as Torryn and Connor were settled in the SUV, he asked her about that.

"I only agreed to a short-term rental," she said. "The owners hoped I would change my mind, but when they heard I would be leaving at the end of the summer, they decided to begin searching for a more permanent tenant."

Sitting in front of the store, Matthew decided to be honest. "I don't want you to go," he whispered, mindful of Connor in the rear seat.

"Don't make this harder than it has to be," Torryn said. "I've been clear with my intentions from the beginning and that hasn't changed."

"We're going to miss you," Matthew said.

"You'll be fine," she countered gently, placing a hand on his arm. "Connor has made friends in town and his nightmares have ceased. Once he starts pre-K, I'll be a distant memory." Her voice hitched and she looked out the window.

"This isn't just about Connor."

"I get that. But why mess with the status quo?" she asked, her voice strained.

"Because I want more. Connor deserves more."

"I agree with you. But I can't be that person."

His cell rang and he answered, happy to be distracted from this upsetting conversation. It was his assistant calling to tell him that a piece of certified mail had been delivered. "I'll swing by and pick it up." They made their way back to his office, the air tense between them. By the time he grabbed the envelope and returned to the SUV, Matthew had had a pep talk with himself. He wasn't going to ruin the good vibes between them by pushing the issue. He would enjoy her company and wish her well when it was time to part ways.

When he reentered the vehicle, Torryn gave him an apologetic look. "I don't want to argue with you."

He squeezed her hand. "I don't want that, either. Just forget I said anything."

After a brief hesitation, she nodded and settled into her seat. Matthew started up the SUV and they departed for his house. For the next few hours, they had a grand time with Connor, each of them bouncing on the trampoline.

Matthew got a kick out of watching Connor dance, recording several videos of his antics on his phone. He also took pictures of Torryn and when she caught him doing it, she made all kinds of silly faces that made him laugh until his stomach hurt. Overall, it was a wonderful afternoon. They put Connor to bed together that night—at Connor's insistence. The only thing he didn't do was kiss her before she left for home.

"I think it's best that we maintain boundaries so that come August, it'll be easier to say goodbye." He doubted that would be the reality, but the more time they spent together, the hope in his heart increased.

She touched his face. "I understand. You need a woman who is deserving of you, Matthew."

"A woman like you, you mean?" he asked.

"If only…" She shook her head and crossed the field to the guesthouse. He waited until she was by her door before going inside his home. Closing the door behind him, Matthew sighed, disliking the quiet. He missed her gregariousness. Her zeal for life.

The sound of the fountain waterfall did nothing to soothe the unease building within him. He pulled out his treadmill from his office closet and dusted it off. But after running a mile, he stepped off, cleaned up, then put on a pair of pajama pants and a T-shirt. Roaming the house, he checked on Connor before wandering into his kitchen.

Matthew moved the curtain at the window to glance over at the guesthouse. All the lights were off except one. Right away, he wanted to text Torryn and see what she was doing. To see if she wanted to chat. It was only 9:00 p.m. His eyes fell on the certified mail that he had left on the counter.

He ripped it open and scanned the document as he went to get a bottle of water from the refrigerator. Blake Whitlock could not accept defeat and now he was coming after Torryn with a trivial case. Oh, he was so angry on Torryn's behalf. He slammed the refrigerator hard and reached for his cell phone. Are you asleep?

Not yet. Drinking tea.

Can you come over? Something came up regarding Ruth's property.

Be right there.

He paced the house until he heard the lock click. The scent of baby powder filled the air. Torryn was also dressed in pink-and-white polka-dot pajamas. "What's going on? Is it the bank?"

"No. Blake Whitlock has filed a case about the property line."

"What? It's five measly inches."

"Believe it or not, as far as property lines go, it is a big deal. I just hoped he wouldn't push the issue."

She put a hand on her hip. "So what does this mean?"

He read the documents. "They've set a date for a month from now."

"A month." She sucked in her breath. "How is that enough time to contest that? Mom's land is practically a landmark."

"Did you come across the house specs when you were cleaning up?"

She shook her head. "No. But I wasn't exactly looking for it. I'll search for them tomorrow." She raised troubled eyes to his. "Not even twenty-four hours and there's another fire to put out."

"Blake will have to come up with more than hearsay to win the case. All will be well."

"Are you able to represent me?"

"I will…but I don't think it's going to come to that."

"I'm going to tell Tess and Nigel about this. Maybe

they might have an idea where I can locate the original deed."

"I'll do some digging on my end as well. I'll reach out to a colleague I know to see if he can locate them in the archives." Matthew patted her arm. "You've come too far for this to be a setback. Look at it as an annoying fly that needs swatting."

Despite her worry, she chuckled. "I just had an image of a fly buzzing around Blake's head."

Matthew cracked up. "How do you do that?" he mused. "How do you manage to laugh in spite of the troubling times?"

She folded her arms. "It's nothing but God."

A piece of paper on the floor caught his eye. It was Connor's drawing. It must have fallen when he shut the door too hard. He picked it up and searched for the magnet. Just as he was about to put it on the door, he saw print on the back.

"No…" he breathed out. "It can't be…" He stood frozen until Torryn came by his side.

"What is it?"

Matthew flipped over the paper in disbelief. "It was there all this time and I didn't know it."

"What? What was there?"

He held up the paper. Goose bumps popped up on his flesh. "The paternity-test results. It was right here behind Connor's sunflowers this whole time."

Torryn trailed behind Matthew into his office. He stuffed the paper in his drawer and slammed it shut.

"I don't get it. You've been hunting for it all this time and you aren't even going to read it?"

"Nope." He jutted his jaw. "I don't need to."

"You must." Her chest heaved. "Connor needs to know his true heritage. You can't hide that from him. It's like burying a bone in the backyard and then kidding yourself into thinking it's no longer there."

"I'm his father."

"Yes, but if you aren't his biological parent, that's something that shouldn't be withheld from Connor."

"We're talking about a four-year-old here. Do you honestly think he's going to understand?"

"Not fully. But being adopted myself, I knew Ruth hadn't given birth to me, but I knew she loved me. I accepted her because of the love she showed me."

"That's all fine and good for you, but I was there for Connor's birth. No test is going to tell me otherwise."

She flailed her hands. "Then why did you get a paternity test in the first place?"

"Because my mother and grandmother kept on about it until I caved."

"I don't buy that." He straightened and squared his shoulders, like a fierce stallion. It was a good thing she wasn't afraid of horses. "The man I have come to know wouldn't have taken that test if deep down a part of you truly didn't want to know."

"You don't know what you're talking about, so I suggest we quit this conversation and you worry about what's going on in your own house and leave me to mine." He stormed out of the office.

She was on his heels. "I'm not going anywhere. As your friend, it's my duty to speak my mind, especially since Connor can't defend himself."

"And why would Connor need defending?" he growled.

"What do you think I'm going to do to him if he's not my son?"

"That's not what I meant. Don't switch up the conversation. If you aren't his father, that's not something that should be kept hidden from him."

"You think you know what's best for my son?" he snarled. "You have a lot of nerve when you're planning to leave him at the end of the summer."

"Oh, no, you're not turning around this argument on me. You're raging like a bull in the pen because deep down you know I'm right." She went into his personal space. "The reason you won't look at that paternity test is because you're scared."

His mouth dropped open. "I'm not scared of the truth."

"Yes, you very much are." She glared at him. "This isn't about Connor. It's about you and your selfishness."

"Self—selfishness?" He backed up. "I can't believe you would say that when I've spent hours and hours helping you."

"Listen, I didn't force you to assist me. You offered. So don't throw that in my face."

For a moment they stood there, saying nothing, neither backing down. Then she exhaled and tried again. "If another man is Connor's father, it won't change your place in his life. It won't change what you mean to him."

"Yes. It would." For a second, she saw the vulnerability in his eyes but then he hardened. "I don't expect you to understand because you don't like responsibility. You grab on to any excuse to avoid anything of substance." He curled his lips. "You have no right telling me what I should or shouldn't do."

Clutching her stomach, she didn't stop the tears from flowing down her cheeks. "Say what you will about me but at least I'm honest about what I think I can do. You're too afraid of losing Connor to face your fears. The truth always comes out. There's no hiding it."

He lifted his chin. "How's this for facing the inevitable? Tonight is your last night watching Connor. Preschool starts mid-August and that's just a few weeks away. I'll manage until then."

Her gut twisted. "You would do that?"

He folded his arms. "Better now than later. You're planning on leaving soon, anyway, so what's the difference?"

"Fine. I'll come by to say goodbye in the morning."

"Don't bother."

"Don't do this," she pleaded, her heart breaking. "I don't want Connor to think I deserted him. That would be cruel."

"You're right. I don't want to cause my son any unnecessary pain." His shoulders slumped. "Okay, you can stop in tomorrow morning. But keep it brief."

With a nod, she fetched the key out of her pocket and placed it on the kitchen counter. "I know you're in papabear mode, but I hope when you've calmed, you'll see that everything I said is because I care." A memory made her cover her mouth. "I promised Connor we would go bike riding tomorrow. Please let me keep my promise."

"That won't be necessary. I'll take him myself."

"Okay." Her chin wobbled. "D-don't forget to wa-water the s-s-sunflowers."

She raced across the lawn back over to the guesthouse. Then she fell to the floor and sobbed. Her body shuddered under the force of her tears as she imagined Connor asking for her, looking for her, and she wouldn't be there. That knowledge crushed her heart. Not to mention she was breaking a promise to Connor. Something she said she would never do.

Chapter Fifteen

"Thanks for coming by to help me, Tess," Torryn said as the sisters huddled on the couch in the main house as they rifled through the plastic bins that they had packed up before. When she contacted her siblings about the property case, Tess had said she would be over the first thing the next morning.

Nigel had texted that he would be in Ryder Hill in a couple of days to go to the court to put in an appeal. With Matthew no longer involved with her, she was glad for her brother and sister's presence.

From her spot on the porch, while she waited for her sister's arrival, she had seen Matthew and Connor leave, jumping into his SUV. Torryn had yearned to join them but she had kept out of sight, not wanting to upset Connor even more.

Her sister studiously ignored her swollen face and reddened eyes, a result of her crying most of the night and this morning. Torryn knew parting ways with Connor would be painful, but she had grossly underestimated the extent of her feelings for him. Her heart felt like it had been gashed open with a hacksaw and she had finally confided as much to her sister.

When she had gone over to tell Connor goodbye a couple hours ago, he had taken it well, beamed at her and said, "Okay, Miss Torryn. See you later." Connor had kissed her cheek with the confidence of someone who expected her to be there. He hadn't understood that their time together had ended. And he was probably thinking they were going on their bike ride today.

Torryn had raced home and broken down. She had wept. Then she had wept even more. Thinking about it even now, tears welled. She sniffled.

"That baby boy got to you, didn't he?" Tess said, looking up from the papers on her lap.

She wiped her face. "I… I feel like a part of me is gone."

Tess said, "Quit it. You are so dramatic." She pointed in the direction of Matthew's place. "Get your butt up and get over there and fix things."

"I—I can't." She sunk into the couch, papers falling to the floor. "Matthew made it very clear that he didn't want me in their lives anymore."

"Why?"

She couldn't talk about the paternity test that led up to the argument since she wasn't going to break Matthew's confidence. But she could share their other matter of contention. "He wants me to settle here, commit to being a permanent part of Connor's life. Of both their lives."

Tess leaned forward. "He's in love with you?"

"He didn't say as much, but he's acting like that could be the case." She shrugged. "I don't know. I've never found myself in this position before so I don't have a frame of reference."

"What position?" Tess cocked her head. "Did something happen between you two?"

"We kissed."

"Ah. So there *is* something between you."

"Yes, but I don't want to put a name on it. I don't want to say it out loud. It makes it more real."

"And your crying all night doesn't?"

"I'm crying because he was mean to me, Tess. He forced me to make a choice."

"What do you expect, Torryn? This isn't just about him. Matthew is a parent. He has a son to worry about. A son who is quite attached to you, I might add. Have you ever thought about how difficult it will be for Connor when you're gone?"

"He's young. He'll forget me eventually." Even as she spoke the words, she knew they weren't true.

"I'm surprised at you." Tess folded her arms. "You were only two years older than Connor is when you lost your mother, and you still remember so much about her."

"You're right." She covered her face with her hands. Connor had to be asking for her and she had no idea what Matthew was telling him. Connor could be quite determined when he wanted something. "I've made a muck of things, haven't I? I am every bit as selfish as I accused Matthew of being."

"You called him selfish?" Tess said, sounding eager for details.

"And he told me that I run from responsibility." She splayed her hands. "Even though I have been taking good care of his child."

"I think you've done a marvelous job but you are a flight risk. A rolling stone." Her sister raised an eyebrow. "You are the most talented person I know. Gifted. Anything you put your mind to, you accomplish, but you never allow yourself to get to the finish line. You always self-sabotage and I have no idea why."

"Because nothing is permanent. Everything is fleeting and disappointments are inevitable. The minute I depend on someone, something happens. Look at Mom. One minute she was there and the next. . ." She swallowed. "I can't put myself out there like that again. I won't."

"Accidents happen, Torryn. There's no avoiding that. But that's no excuse not to live. One of the happiest I've seen you is when you're baking. Your fundraiser in Mom's honor was a big success because you have mad skills. So why not build on that? You're getting older and you'll want to plant seeds toward a proper retirement. You don't want to be in your eighties and hustling because you didn't invest your time wisely. Like you said, life is fleeting and you don't want to be caught unawares."

"You're gifted at throwing my own words back at me, you know that?"

"Is it working?" she asked.

"I promise I'll give your advice some thought. Now, let's get back to finding this paperwork." She stood and went into the bathroom to wash her face and compose herself.

When she returned, her sister held up an aged roll of papers. "I think I've found the original blueprints to the house." She jumped to her feet and they rushed into the kitchen, where she could spread them out on the table.

"These are construction drawings," Torryn said, excitement building. "Good job, sis. This could be our breakthrough." The sisters high-fived.

"I don't understand what it all means. Let's send them to Nigel."

Minutes later, Nigel texted. Those aren't for Mom's house.

Deflated, Torryn and Tess looked at each other. "What are we going to do?" Tess asked. "Maybe we should call Matthew…"

She shook her head. "I don't want to bother him. Let's reach out to Blake and see if we can reason with him."

"I don't think he's going to bend, but it's worth a try." Tess pulled out her phone and called Blake to invite him to tea.

"I've got some cobbler in the kitchen."

"If you've got lemons, I'll make lemonade," Tess offered, quirking her lips. The metaphor wasn't lost on either of them.

"How much longer, Daddy?" Connor asked, taking up the rear as they rode their bicycles home. Matthew had led them around the paved path by the pond about two miles away and now they were circling back. "I'm really, really thirsty and my legs are really, really tired."

He had carried a couple bottles of waters but they had finished those by the time they arrived at the pond. "We're almost back at the house, son, and then we can have some water. Later, we'll go out for ice cream."

"Yay!" Connor propelled even faster then, his training wheels clanking against the gravel. "Is Miss Torryn coming with us?"

"No, it will be just me and you."

"Oh…"

That was about the fifth time he had asked for Torryn, and that was just during their bike ride. And she had been the first person he had asked for when he woke up. Every time Matthew answered in the negative, Connor's face dropped and Matthew's guilt grew.

He was responsible for Connor's misery.

A few times Matthew had been tempted to knock on Torryn's door or call and beg her to come back, but then he remembered how she had called him selfish. She hadn't taken that back or apologized. So he backed down. Besides, Torryn was going to leave in a matter of weeks, so what was the point?

Even knowing all that, as they pedaled into the driveway, his eyes searched her property for any sign of her. But he hadn't seen his next-door neighbor since he had put her out of his home. Torryn loved the outdoors so she was actively avoiding him. And Connor.

That knowledge gutted him. He was…miserable. Nothing was the same without her. She made the most mundane task extraordinary and now it was like the light was snuffed out of his life.

Connor wouldn't see his melancholy, though. Over the past weeks, Matthew had packed their daily schedules to the point of exhaustion. They had gone peach picking, driven to Bethany beach and built sand castles and gone to the water park on his off days. When he needed a sitter, he alternated between a couple of teenage girls who had answered his ad, since they were out of school for the summer.

After Matthew and Connor refreshed themselves, Connor shocked him by saying that he didn't want ice cream. He wanted to go play in his room. And he had turned down Matthew's offer to play with him. Instead, that evening they had watered the sunflowers with Connor craning his neck to see if Torryn would show up, which battered Matthew's resolve. Then they had snuggled together in their pj's on the couch and watched TV.

Right before they said their nighttime prayers, Connor sighed and said, "I miss Miss Torryn."

His sigh was like a grater scraping at Matthew's heart. "I miss her, too, son," he admitted, then hugged his son close and kissed the top of his head.

"Daddy, Abe told me he has a new mommy and I wanted to ask if Miss Torryn could be my new mommy?" He looked at Matthew, those hazel eyes earnest and pleading. "Please?"

"Unfortunately, it doesn't work that way, son. Miss Torryn has other things to do, remember? That's why she hasn't been by to visit. She's really busy working on her house."

"Yeah, but she said I could talk to her anytime I want and I just want to talk to her for a little bit." Connor broke into tears.

"Hush, it's going to be okay," Matthew whispered. "Daddy is here."

"Please, Daddy, please." His body shook as he cried.

Calling himself the worst father on the planet, Matthew hoisted Connor in his arms and rubbed his son's back. "I'm here, son. You can talk to me."

"O-k-k-a-ay." Connor dragged out the word, an indication that he was anything but. Matthew drew in a deep breath to keep from falling apart.

Matthew paced the room and sang "It is Well With

My Soul." He sang until Connor's tears reduced to sniffles and then there was nothing but quiet, his body slack with sleep.

Laying Connor back onto his bed, Matthew kissed his son's forehead. "I love you, my son."

Was he, though? Was Connor his son?

He had the means to find out but he was stalling. It hurt to admit it but maybe Torryn was right, and this was all about his own fears.

Well, it was time he faced them.

Matthew marched to the drawer where he had stashed the letter and pulled it open with such force that it came out. He sat with the drawer on his lap and looked at the letter that could change his life. The sunflower drawing was face up.

Seeing it eased the pounding of his heart. Whatever the outcome, he would do all he could to make Connor's future sunny and bright.

Matthew took a deep breath, then flipped over the paper. A few minutes later he surged to his feet.

He was 99.99 percent Connor's father.

Connor was his.

Dropping to his knees, Matthew lifted his hands even as the tears flowed down his face. "God, I thank You and praise You." He stayed in that position for quite some time before rising to go into Connor's room. He needed a moment to soak in his discovery and to take in his son.

His grandmother was right. His mother was right. Garth was right. Torryn was right.

The truth freed him. It was like a breath of fresh air after being inside a hot stuffy space for days, or in this case, years. There would be no more wondering, or guessing. There was just certainty of his place in Connor's life.

And joy. Overwhelming joy! *Thank You, Jesus.* If it wasn't for the dread of dealing with a cranky four-year-old, Matthew would have bellowed into the night. He rushed down the stairs to return Connor's drawing on the refrigerator.

He couldn't wait to tell Torryn the results. She was going to insist they celebrate. Grabbing his phone, Matthew pulled up Torryn's contact info, then paused. He had severed ties with Torryn. They weren't friends. They weren't anything anymore. His exuberance withered like a wet noodle.

Why was Torryn the only person he wanted to call? *You know why.*

The truth blossomed in his chest. He was hopelessly in love with Torryn Emerson. Deep down, he had already known it, but to admit it meant that he would have to do something about it.

What if she rejected him, though? If she rejected him, she rejected him, but he wasn't going to let her leave town without stating his case. And he knew just where to do it.

Chapter Sixteen

Torryn sat between Nigel and Tess in the middle of the courtroom while they waited for their case to come up. The torrential rains outside mirrored her mood and state of mind. It was the perfect backdrop for when they lost this case. Because they surely would.

Knowing today's weather, she had arrived at the courthouse a half hour early so she would have time to make sure her hair and makeup were court-ready. She was dressed in a black dress and a pair of black pumps, with every strand of hair gelled in place.

"We shouldn't be here," Tess whispered under her breath in between cases.

"I agree, but Blake refused to drop his suit," Torryn said. "So we have to fight."

Nigel chimed in. "It's what Mom would want us to do."

"Is Matthew coming?" Tess asked, when the judge called a recess.

Torryn squeezed her hand. "Yes… He said he would." Matthew was too much of a professional to drop the case without proper notice. Plus, his love for her mother was genuine, regardless of how he felt about her. She had lost count of how many times she had replayed when he'd sent her out of his house.

"He'll be here," Nigel said, confident.

Blake strutted in with his attorney, acknowledged them and sat on the opposite side of the courtroom.

Torryn curled her hand around Nigel's arm and squeezed. A few minutes before their case was called, she saw Matthew rush inside with Connor by his side. They were wet, their clothes soaked. Torryn couldn't think of a time she had ever seen Matthew looking so disheveled.

They both came up to her and held up signs.

"What are they doing?" Nigel asked, from behind her. "Why are they holding up fake deeds?"

"Aw, it's the deeds to their hearts," Tess said. "That is the cutest thing I ever saw."

Torryn leaned over to investigate, then gasped. "Oh, my. I love it!" It was the corniest, sweetest thing she had ever seen.

"I love you, Miss Torryn," Connor said. The crowd in the courtroom were oohing and aahing. Nigel had taken out his phone and was recording it all.

She picked Connor up and whirled him around. "I missed you so much."

"I love you, too," Matthew said. "You coming into my life is an answer to a prayer I didn't know I had."

Her mouth popped open. "I—I don't know what to say."

"Are you serious, right now?" Tess jumped to her feet. "You need to say you love them, too."

Torryn leaned down to look Connor in the eyes. "I love you, Connor, and I'll gladly accept the deed to your heart." She looked up at Matthew and whispered, "Yours, too."

Matthew waved a hand. "Hang on a minute." He put the sign down and took out some papers. "I have secured old drawings of the plot of land that dates back to the 1800s." Nigel and Tess came over and they huddled together to take a look. "You'll see that there is an issue with the property line. But it's in your favor. It extends farther into Blake's property."

Once Matthew showed the papers to the judge, the case was quickly dismissed. Blake stopped them in the hallway to ask if they were going to make him move the fence.

"We'll be in touch," Nigel said. If Torryn knew her brother, he was going to make Blake sweat for putting them through this ordeal.

"Now, Mom can finally be at peace," Tess said, then raised an eyebrow. "I trust you'll get a ride home?" She jutted her chin toward Matthew and Connor, who stood waiting for Torryn by the exit.

"I think I'll be fine." Her chest expanded with hope and love. For once in her life she was hopeful for a future.

Nigel kissed Torryn on the cheek. "Handle your business, sis."

Tess gave her a hug. "Don't let love slip away. Grab on to it with all you've got."

She looked over at Matthew and Connor and smiled. "I will."

Epilogue

Where was she? Matthew stood in the driveway tapping his foot and eyeing his watch every few seconds.

It was close to 5:00 p.m. and Torryn had yet to turn the bend. He shouldn't be surprised that she was behind schedule. She had a lot crammed into today, as usual. Today was move-out day from the guesthouse and the grand opening of her bakery, but she had insisted on picking Connor up from his first day of preschool.

He heard the screech of the tires before Torryn's car came into view. Cupping his mouth, he yelled, "Show-off." Ever since she had gotten her driver's license last month, she had been speeding on the backstreets. Practicing and honing her skills. He wasn't worried, though, because Torryn was a safe driver. That screech around the curve had been for his entertainment. He knew she was holding the wheel at ten and two the entire way home.

Torryn came to a smooth stop in front of the house, then she rolled down the window. "Been waiting long?" He rolled his eyes. She was such a tease. And he liked it.

"It's about time you got here." He leaned down to open the passenger door and help Connor out of his car seat. "I've been waiting for this moment for weeks."

All she did was quirk her lips, her eyes alight with mischief. She had enjoyed stretching his patience for sure.

"Hello, Daddy." Connor bounced over to him, his backpack flapping on his back. "I had fun at school today."

"That's great. I can't wait to hear all about it. Now, go inside and wash your hands. I left a special treat for you on the table."

Torryn reached for his hand. "Don't you want to go inside, too?"

Matthew dug in his heels. "No. I need to hear you say those words now."

Torryn grew serious. Her eyes filled with tenderness. "Matthew, I held off on saying these three words because there were a few things I had to do for me first. As the saying goes, you have to love yourself before you can love others."

His heart moved. "Oh, sweetheart, you don't—"

She put her hand on his chest. "Let me finish." At his nod, she continued. "I didn't feel worthy. Even though my mother believed in me, I had to believe in myself. And so I had to make some changes. First, I had to stop running. That's why I worked hard to get my official pastry certification and to secure the lease on the bakery." She touched his face. "The only running I plan on doing from now on is running after Connor and running toward you."

His arms went around her waist and he drew her close.

"Second, I had to face my fear of driving and get my driver's license. I thank you for your help getting me back behind the wheel. I aced the driving test and managed to take a decent photo at the DMV." They laughed.

"That's a major accomplishment because mine's hideous," he joked.

"And finally, I finished my time on Mom's property and got her house cleaned up and fully cleared out for my brother's arrival." She took a deep breath, then exhaled. "I finished quite a few things that I started, so that when I tell you that I love you, you'll know that I mean every word because I am a woman of my word."

"I love you, too. I love the woman that you are, and Connor and I will be right by your side cheering you on through your next achievement."

"That's all great to hear, but I didn't tell you that I love you yet." Her eyes sparkled.

"You are so right." Matthew laughed. "You sure didn't. I can see that you're going to make me laugh every day."

"Matthew Lawson, I love you with all of my heart. I thank you for opening your heart to me. I hope you'll open your home, your life and give me the best gift I could ever ask for." Her eyes welled. Then she cupped his face with her hands. "If you'll have me, I'll be the best mother I can to your son that I possibly can be."

Matthew grabbed her close again and kissed her with all the love he had for her in his heart. It wasn't until Connor called out that he broke the kiss.

"Come see, Daddy. Come see." Connor dashed to the front of the house. He and Torryn followed closely behind. He heard a gasp and then Torryn froze. He followed her line of vision. When he saw what stood before him, he couldn't hold the tears. A single sunflower stood majestic, opened and in bloom.

"It's a sunflower, Daddy. You see it, Daddy?" Connor hopped around, circling Matthew and Torryn.

He looked over at Torryn standing beside him and his heart expanded. "Yes, I see it, son. I really do."

* * * * *

Dear Reader,

I am so grateful for the opportunity to write these stories of love and hope for Love Inspired. The blessing of being able to do so comes right along with my toughest trial. My son has been struggling, and as a mother I wish I could take his pain away. I've been praying and asking God to remove it completely. But sometimes, God chooses not to, and you have so many questions until you circle back around to who God is and His faithfulness.

While writing Matthew and Torryn's story, the song "Great is Thy Faithfulness" got me through so much. Matthew had a lot of past hurt from his late wife's betrayal, and Torryn was afraid to love because of great loss in her life, but they were able to find each other. Two hurting souls who were reminded of God's faithfulness and the power of love. When we open our hearts to love, it really does heal so much pain and sorrow.

I hope you enjoyed the beauty of their story as I did. The theme of forgiveness is also prevalent throughout. None of us are perfect. We all come short. Matthew had to forgive his wife and Torryn had to forgive herself so that they could receive all the good that God meant for them and so that they were ready for the love of their heart.

I would love to hear your thoughts. Please connect with me on social media and check out my other books at www.zoeymariejackson.com.

Warmly,
Zoey Marie

Harlequin® Reader Service

Enjoyed your book?

Try the perfect subscription for Romance readers and get more great books like this delivered right to your door.

See why over 10+ million readers have tried Harlequin Reader Service.

Start with a Free Welcome Collection with free books and a gift—valued over $20.

Choose any series in print or ebook. See website for details and order today:

TryReaderService.com/subscriptions